TO
AVRIL

Wishy yo
"thrilly Red.

+ +

Nancy

THE INCEPTOR TRILOGY
VOLUME 1
THE SPIRIT

THE INCEPTOR TRILOGY
VOLUME 1
THE SPIRIT

Maureen Farenden

Book Guild Publishing
Sussex, England

First published in Great Britain in 2006 by
Book Guild Publishing
25 High Street
Lewes, East Sussex
BN7 2LU

Typesetting in Baskerville by
Keyboard Services, Luton, Bedfordshire

Printed in Great Britain by
CPI Bath

A catalogue record for this book is available from
The British Library

ISBN 1 84624 042 5

Contents

1

The Spirit

All is dark and quiet as I lay stretched out in my comfy king-sized bed secretly enjoying all the space, which is usually occupied by my wonderful but rather larger other half Monty, who is still away at our other house in Somerset. Just as I am savouring this delicious moment the door opens with its usual force and in enters Aunt Lizzy, my housekeeper and younger sister of my beloved Ma, who passed away 30 years ago, but whose spirit is with me every day. A powerhouse of a woman who's still vibrant at 60 years plus, with her wild grey Irish hair surrounding her rosy round face. Her porcelain skin now cracked and lined by the passage of time. Her 5ft frame once so petite now as wide as the door she enters.

'Will yah be getting yourself out of bed, darling,' she bellows in her strong Irish brogue (even though she's been away from the 'old country' for nearly 40 years), as she makes her way towards the window to draw the curtains, pulling my bed covers off at the same time in her usual 'no time to waste' manner. Within seconds my beautiful, dark, peaceful world is evaporated into the cold light of day. I love my big, loud, oh so soft Aunt dearly, but at moments like this I could cheerfully throttle her.

As I stretch out and begin to open my eyes to take in the first light of the day, my mind awakens from its cosy slumber and immediately hungers for the adventures of a new day. I glance at the clock on my bedside table – it's 7.00 a.m. – while thinking to myself what an unusually good night's sleep I had. Being an insomniac since childhood, I often get up at around 4.00 a.m. and potter around the house. Sometimes after having one of my psychic dreams I get up and go to my quiet room to analyse it.

As Aunt Lizzy buzzes around my bedroom I slowly make my way to the bathroom.

'Don't yah be long now, darling, the day is dwindling already and breakfast needs to be eaten fresh,' shouts Aunt Lizzy, as she hastily makes her way back to the kitchen.

Once again I stare into the bathroom mirror and ponder the face that looks back at me. The straight blond hair, deep blue (laughing!) eyes according to my Monty, pale freckly skin with yet another fresh laughter line that's sneaked in overnight. I stretch my lips to reveal what is considered one of my best features, according to Aunt Lizzy: 'good strong white teeth'. Ah well, what is fresh faced youth compared to the classic beauty of the mature woman? My favourite words to myself each morning since I reached the age of 40.

Forty-five minutes later I stare back into my full-length bedroom mirror to see Charity Holmes, born Charity Merrick, the working-class girl from the East End, of Irish parents, who has, as they say, 'made good'. My freckles masterly disguised under the mask of make-up, with my petite, curvy frame cleverly hidden in my favourite black cashmere top, skirt, soft black leather boots and jewellery to complete the illusion. Hmm, if only I was three inches taller, one stone lighter and five years younger I'd be almost perfect. But then perfection has its downside. But with 45 minutes of careful preparation now complete I'm ready to take on the world. Oh how I love the dawn of each new day and the thrill and excitement of the new adventures and challenges that come with it.

'Will yah get into the kitchen, darling, and eat this breakfast before it grows moss,' yells Aunty Lizzy.

'Good morning,' are the soft words that greet me as I enter my large country-style kitchen. The greeting comes courtesy of Robyn, my trusted niece and secretary, the daughter of my beloved late older sister Annie, whose early death at the age of 32, from the same illness that took my beloved Ma at 34, still casts a dark shadow over my world. Robyn looks so like Annie when she was 22 with that willowy frame, long, silky black hair, large dark brown eyes and flawless pale Irish skin, with that gentle voice that belies her steely character underneath.

'You're in early today, Robyn. I didn't think I had any appointments until this afternoon, so thought you had the morning off.'

'I did. But for some strange reason I felt this uncontrollable compulsion to come into the office early. I can't explain why.'

'Hmm... I'm intrigued already.'

'Well, when I arrived at the office at the ungodly hour of six the telephone rang the minute I entered the room and then it began.'

'What began? What began?' pipes in Aunt Lizzy, who by now has stopped cooking breakfast and is listening intently to Robyn.

'I picked up the telephone to hear this deep, rather slow voice, with what sounded like a Southern American drawl. "This is Mr Stephen Mallon, am I speaking to Charity Holmes?" "No," I reply. "Miss Holmes is unavailable at the moment. Can I help you? I'm her secretary, Robyn Marlow."'

By this time both Aunt Lizzy and I are hanging on Robyn's every word.

' "It's imperative that I see Charity Holmes this morning," he says angrily. I informed him that this wasn't possible and looked in the diary to suggest an alternative date while asking the reason for his call. He suddenly became very agitated, stating that he'd flown in from America with the sole purpose of seeing you. Then it happened.'

'What happened? What happened?' yells Aunt Lizzy, all excited.

'Calm down, calm down, Lizzy, let Robyn continue,' I say, appearing to be in control but already my psychic powers, which I've had since childhood, are warning me that I'm about to embark on what will become one of the darkest and most evil investigations of my career.

Robyn continues. 'As I tried to ascertain more information from him I suddenly felt this intense icy-cold presence around me in the room.'

'Did it feel as if he was actually in the room with you while you were talking to him?' I ask, worried at what evil spirit may have manifested itself into my home.

'Yes, it felt exactly like that. I'm absolutely convinced he was in the room, yet I couldn't see him, just feel this incredible presence.'

'Oh bejesus, bejesus protect us our good Lord,' Aunt Lizzy cries while doing her usual sign of the cross.

'Did you feel threatened by his presence in any way? Was his anger directed at you or an expression of his own feelings?' I ask, trying to establish what this spirit was seeking from me.

'No, it was a strange sensation almost as if he was attempting to get to you through me. He kept repeating over and over again that he needed to speak to you,' Robyn replies.

'So let me clarify this. You were speaking to him on the telephone, but at the same time you're positive that you could feel his presence in the room with you?'

'Yes, absolutely. His manner on the telephone was that of a powerful man, who was cold and distant. Yet I sensed desperation, even vulnerability in his voice, as if his world had just crumbled. I found myself confirming an appointment for him to see you here today at ten-thirty.'

'What happened once you confirmed the appointment?'

'The phone line went dead before I could get a contact number or address from him, and the office suddenly seemed free of this oppressive presence.'

'Oh my sweet Lord, this is not good, not good at all,' says Aunt Lizzy, now more quiet and thoughtful in both her manner and voice, but still doing her usual sign of the cross.

'Since you came to stay with me last year, Robyn, your "gift" has grown stronger and stronger. But your psychic powers are weak and still in their infancy. The spirit knows this but can still use your earthly body to connect with me.'

'Why not simply contact you direct? Why use me when you're already in the house and your psychic powers are much stronger than mine? Why speak to me through the telephone and not in the room when I felt his presence around me?'

'Ah, Robyn, darling, the world of the spirit moves in its own way,' says Aunt Lizzy quietly.

'What time was it when you felt this uncontrollable need to come to the office so early?' I ask, even though my gift is already warning me to be prepared.

'I was having trouble sleeping so got up around four and made myself a hot drink to help me relax. But for some strange reason I felt agitated and very restless and suddenly found myself getting ready for work even though I knew I had the morning off. I just couldn't stop myself, but at the same time knew it was ridiculous.'

'At around four I was in such a deep sleep that the

5

doorway between the spirit world and earthly plain wasn't open.'

'What's this "doorway"? I've never heard you mention it before?' Robyn asks, eager to learn more.

'Only the chosen few experience what is known as "psychic dreams" in which souls from the spirit world can enter through the doorway into your dreams. But they can only enter when the medium or psychic they've chosen is still semi-conscious and not in a deep sleep when the doorway is closed. Mr Mallon, who I suspect is in spirit, must have been trying to contact me through the doorway. As I was in an unusually deep sleep last night he was unable to gain entry so looked for another means of access, in this case you, Robyn.'

'How are psychic dreams different from the normal dreams?' asks Robyn, who by now is listening intently.

'These dreams are very profound. When I experience one I often feel very cold and detached as if I've been invited by the soul or energy from spirit to merely observe. Even though I feel detached from what's going on in the dream I can still see, hear, taste and smell everything around me. They're never straightforward and sometimes very frightening. The message that's sent within them is often very complex and hard to unravel. They often serve as premonitions or warnings of impending danger. These dreams must be adhered to, as failure to read the signs result in the dream becoming reality. In this instance it appears that his need to see or speak to me was so urgent that he had to go through another doorway. As you were awake he chose you.'

'But why did I end up making an appointment for him to see you at ten-thirty this morning? Why not just appear to you now that you're awake if he needs to see or speak to you that urgently?'

'That's the intriguing question and one that we'll have

6

to wait to find out,' I say, making light of the situation to Robyn and Aunt Lizzy, though secretly I am worried. For indeed Robyn is right. Why the unusual scenarios of the telephone call resulting in an appointment to see me? Spirits don't make appointments – they appear as and when it suits their needs or when they've been 'summoned' by other means.

Even I, Charity Holmes, famous psychic investigator, internationally known as the Inceptor, can sense that this is a bad omen.

From the age of five years old I experienced feelings, voices and visions, which I had no control of yet kept secret, as I instinctively knew I was different from my friends and family. Then at the age of ten my beloved Ma, during the last six months of her life, told me the history of our family and the powerful gift within me. The gift that's been passed down to a selected few in the Merrick family, skipping generations along the way, sleeping as Ma would say, only to come back with a vengeance and even stronger in me. Ma and my sister Annie didn't have the gift, neither does Aunt Lizzy. But my great-grandmother did and so does Robyn, who has come to stay with me in order to learn how to both control and understand this powerful force that is now growing within her. This very same gift that has both comforted and sometimes tormented me over the years, whose power, if not used correctly and wisely, can cause as much pain as pleasure. Before my beloved Ma passed away, she helped me to understand this powerful force within me and began to show me how to both control and use it as a force for good. She taught me how to channel my gift by using various methods and tools to use my psychic powers to their fullest potential. I've spent many years studying the mantic arts and gone back through history to achieve this, and I continue on this journey of knowledge every day.

It was my destiny to become an inceptor (the name given to those with exceptional psychic powers who have the ability to intercept between the living here on earth and those in spirit).

Over the years I've experienced such wonders. I've been called upon to use my psychic powers in many situations in my career as an inceptor, which I prefer to call a vocation. My clients are not only from the living but also from the spirit world, which I've no control over and must respond to. Although they don't like to admit it, the police often call upon me to use my psychic powers when they are unable to solve a case. I give lectures all over the world on psychic phenomena and hold seminars on many subjects including mediumship, psychic ability, the psychology of our dreams. I also hold classes and teach on the mantic arts.

With my psychic powers and gift of 'clear seeing' (the ability to see deep into the minds of others), I've now gained quite a reputation.

We could leave the house before 10.30, but experience has taught me that there is nowhere to hide or run to when the spirit has sought you out. Aunt Lizzy and Robyn know that whatever fears I have, nothing will stop me now from keeping that appointment with the mysterious Mr Mallon.

I check my watch. The time is 8.30 a.m. and I contemplate the things I wanted to do this morning. Ring Monty and write some letters, telephone my dearest and oldest friend Sam (short for Samantha). I decide that the letters can wait but Monty and Sam are a must.

'Right, you two, we'll go about business as usual and await the presence of Mr Mallon.'

'Oh Lord. Oh Lord. I'll be doing some strong praying this morning,' whispers Aunt Lizzy under her breath, appearing nervous, but past experience has proven that she'll fight to the death to protect her beloved nieces. Aunt Lizzy has never married, and promised both my sister Annie and Ma to love and protect us as if we were her own children. A promise she'll never relinquish. Then, suddenly, I have a thought, and ask Robyn: 'Have you had any other calls on the office line since the one from the mysterious Mr Mallon?'

'No,' she replies, slightly puzzled.

'Perhaps it might be an idea to dial 1471 and see where the call originated from. You never know, there may even be a real telephone number with an address to go with it.'

'Why didn't I think of that? What an idiot I am.'

'It's not every day you get a visit from the "other side" so don't be so hard on yourself. In fact I think you've done remarkably well under the circumstances,' I reply gently.

'To be sure, you are right there, darling, I don't think I'd be so calm as to just sit down and eat breakfast after talking with what appears to be a ghost and him being an American as well,' Aunt Lizzy pipes in while clearing away the breakfast dishes.

I make my way along the hallway towards my quiet room, where everyone knows not to enter when the sign outside says QUIET TIME – NO ENTRY.

It's my favourite room because it's where I go to have my own space, where I can do or be anything I want. I sit in my big comfy leather armchair and simply daydream or dip into happy memories, thinking of Ma or my beloved Monty. I can get lost in time. Reading my books, continuing my research into psychic phenomena and the mantic arts, analyse my psychic dreams, consult the ancient tarot and write my lectures and letters. Spend ages chatting to Monty on the telephone when he's away and my best friend Sam. It's a room where I'm surrounded by my many treasures, which I've collected on my journeys around the world and where I truly feel at peace.

Robyn goes to the office to dial 1471 to see if she can trace the telephone number and origin of our mysterious caller. Aunt Lizzy goes to her bedroom to get her treasured rosary beads, apparently blessed by the Pope himself, to pray. She would normally do this at night before going to bed, but always throws in extra prayers when she decides her nieces need that little bit of extra help from above.

Suddenly I feel the same intense presence around me that Robyn described when talking to the mysterious Mr Mallon. As I get closer and closer to my quiet room this feeling intensifies. It's both menacing and yet strangely vulnerable. I immediately sense that it's a person who's in spirit but their aura is so cold that I feel they've only just left the living.

'Who are you and what are you seeking from me?'

'You must be careful; they'll not let you find my secret.'

The voice is deep and strong with an American accent that has a slow drawl, which I can't place yet somehow know I've heard before.

'Is that you, Mr Mallon? What secret? Who are they? Who are you? And why have you chosen me?' I ask in quick succession, while trying to contain my fear. For if there is one thing I'm sure of above all else it's that the world of spirit can be more dangerous and unpredictable than any other force and more so when the spirit seeks you out. As I turn around in the hallway I feel the anger from this spirit is so intense that it almost renders me frozen. Yet I instinctively know that it's not directed at me, but the sense of menace and hatred is incredibly strong. Suddenly I hear the sound of someone breathing and feel their icy-cold breath on my face followed by the same words again.

'You must be careful; they'll not let you find my secret.'

Before I can utter another word, the spirit is gone, but I know he'll return. When they've chosen to seek you out and you haven't gone searching for them, they'll not rest until their request has been granted. I turn to open the door, feeling an even stronger desire than normal for the safe haven of my quiet room.

Suddenly Robyn rushes into the room. 'I've traced the telephone number for Mr Mallon.'

At the same time Aunt Lizzy comes rushing in. 'I felt something pass me in the hallway when I was on the way to the bathroom, yet I couldn't see anybody. Are you both all right?'

'Why, what's happened?' Robyn asks quickly.

'I've just been visited by Mr Mallon, only this time it wasn't by telephone. He was in the hallway. I could hear his voice and feel his breath on my face, but he didn't materialise. I sensed he wasn't long in spirit.'

'What did he say?' Robyn and Aunt Lizzy ask almost simultaneously.

'He said: "You must be careful; they'll not let you find my secret." He said it twice and before I could ask him any more questions he was gone.'

'Well, you're right about him not being long in spirit,' Robyn replies.

'What have you found out?' I ask.

'I traced the telephone number to the Dorchester Hotel here in London. When I telephoned to speak to Mr Mallon, the receptionist on the desk informed me that he was found dead in his hotel room at six this morning. She stated that he requested an early morning call for this time and was most insistent that the receptionist on duty made the call. So when Mr Mallon didn't answer his telephone, the hotel porter was sent to wake him up only to discover him stabbed to death in his bed. The

11

hotel security immediately called the police who apparently have found no murder weapon or clues as to who the murderer is. The receptionist went on to say that Mr Mallon booked in alone at seven the previous evening, dined alone that night and appeared to have no visitors. When she asked me what my connection to Mr Mallon was I told her that we'd received a call from him at six this morning. She sounded shocked, stating that this couldn't be possible, because although Mr Mallon was found dead at six, police forensics have confirmed the time of death at approximately four this morning.'

Just as the three of us are trying to comprehend everything that's happened the front door bell rings.

2

Cloak of Death

As the three of us stand frozen in time for what seems like ages the front door bell continues to ring. I look at the clock on my desk – the time is 9.15 a.m.

'You'd better see who's at the door, Lizzy,' I say, moving towards my desk.

As Aunt Lizzy opens the door she's faced with two stern men.

'Is this the home of Charity Holmes?' the first man enquires. He's very plump, middle-aged with a badly fitting toupee and tiny moustache. His voice is gruff and quick, almost as if time to him is at a premium and every second has to be allocated and accounted for.

'Who are you and what do you require from Miss Holmes?' Aunt Lizzy asks sharply.

'I'm Chief Inspector Cranky (a name that seemed to suit his personality precisely), and I need to speak to Miss Holmes urgently in connection with a murder that took place in the early hours of this morning.'

Aunt Lizzy stares blankly at the Inspector, controlling her emotions, as past experience has taught her never to reveal her feelings to outsiders.

'What's that got to do with Miss Holmes?' enquires Aunt Lizzy, putting on her aloof, slightly superior Irish accent, the one she uses for people she takes an instant dislike to.

'I'd prefer to discuss the matter direct with Miss Holmes,' replies the Chief Inspector as he pushes his way past, with his sidekick Sergeant Dredge (another apt name) following in quick succession. A highly nervous, much younger man with thick brown hair and a wiry thin frame, which twitches every time the Chief Inspector speaks.

'Well, you'd better be coming this way then as you seem to have no manners in waiting for the proper introductions,' snaps Aunt Lizzy as she shows both Cranky and Dredge (a right old pair of miseries, she mutters under her breath) into the quiet room.

'Charity, my darling, this is Chief Inspector Cranky and Sergeant Dredge who insist on seeing you urgently without an appointment,' growls Aunt Lizzy while fixing her 'step out of line and I'll kneecap the both of you' look at them.

'Are you Charity Holmes, the so-called psychic investigator?' asks the Chief Inspector.

'Well, you've got me there, Chief Inspector, I'm her. How can I help you?' I reply with my usual light-hearted banter, for I'm used to being spoken of and to in a derogatory manner by the police. Over the years I've found it best to ignore their attempts to diminish who I am, and my gift, for they inevitably return for my help.

'I'm investigating the death of an American named Stephen Mallon, who was found brutally murdered this morning in his hotel bedroom. On checking his diary it appears he'd an appointment with you this morning at ten-thirty. Can you tell me in what connection you knew Mr Mallon and the reason for his appointment with you this morning?'

Hmm, this is going to be interesting, I think to myself, as I ponder on how I am going to explain to the Chief Inspector an appointment made with a man already dead.

Somehow I don't need to use my psychic powers to sense that he isn't the type to believe in the spirit world.

'All I can tell you, Chief Inspector, is that Mr Mallon telephoned my office this morning at six and spoke to my secretary, Robyn, to make an appointment to see me urgently. The time agreed was ten-thirty. As to my connection with Mr Mallon, I'm unable at this time to give you an answer as I'm still in the process of seeking one myself.'

The Chief Inspector stares back coldly, unable to hide his irritation at not being given what he considers a direct answer to his question, while Sergeant Dredge is taking notes, twitching and slowly perusing every inch of Robyn from under his notebook. Robyn can feel his eyes upon her and instantly knows there is an opportunity to glean information from him. For if there's one thing Robyn has mastered it's using her beauty, combined with her psychic powers, to devastating effect on men.

'That's very interesting, Miss Holmes. You're telling me that your secretary spoke to Mr Mallon at six this morning yet according to police forensics he was already dead at four. So unless I'm mistaken she was having a conversation with a dead man, who at the same time managed to write down his appointment with you at ten-thirty in his diary. Quite an amazing feat don't you think?' snaps the Chief Inspector, unable to hide both his anger and disbelief.

'The world of spirit moves in its own mysterious way, Chief Inspector, and the spirit of Mr Mallon has chosen my Aunt as his connection here on earth. Why, we've yet to unravel,' Robyn replies rushing to my defence.

'So you're also a psychic then, Miss...?'

'Robyn is my niece, Chief Inspector, and yes she has the gift too and I can assure you that between us we shall discover the truth with regard to Mr Mallon.'

15

'What do you mean by the truth?' Sergeant Dredge asks, twitching and looking puzzled at the same time.

'Mr Mallon informed Robyn that he specifically came to London to see me and somehow Robyn found herself making an appointment for ten-thirty. The fact that he was already dead when the appointment was made and you found it written in his diary, I find particularly interesting. I feel there is a connection between the murder of Mr Mallon at four and his subsequent phone call to my office at six to make that appointment to see me at ten-thirty. I believe these times are intrinsically linked and form the key that will open the door to Mr Mallon's secret and the reason for his murder.'

'What secret?' snarls the Chief Inspector, irritated and annoyed that I seem to know something that his investigations have missed.

'I had a visit from Mr Mallon in spirit, not long before your arrival this morning, Chief Inspector, in which he warned me to be careful, as "they" won't let me find his secret. It's clear to me that I've been chosen to uncover this secret, which I believe is the reason why he was murdered. Mr Mallon's spirit has called upon me to seek both justice and truth for him.'

'Ah, and while this miraculous visitation from the recently departed Mr Mallon was taking place, why not just give you the name of his killer, instead of these cryptic messages about secrets?'

'Life's never that simple, Chief Inspector, either in the spirit world or here on earth, otherwise there'd be no need for either of us now would there? But you can rest assured that as soon as I and my trusted team come across anything significant you'll be the first to know. Now if you don't have any other questions, I've a busy schedule and so bid you good day. Lizzy will show you out.'

16

Aunt Lizzy steps in quickly and shows both Cranky and Dredge the way to the front door, making no attempt to hide her instant dislike of them both.

'We'll be in contact again, Miss Holmes,' shouts the Chief Inspector, looking somewhat dazed and irritated at being dismissed in what he considers an abrupt and disrespectful manner. Sergeant Dredge is hot on his heels, but manages to throw a quick nervous smile at Robyn on his way out. Robyn raises her eyes, while tilting her head back to one side as she throws one of her careful suggestive smiles back at him, knowing this will leave it open for her to pick his brains later.

'Well, I'm glad to be rid of them two miseries,' snaps Aunt Lizzy as she rushes back, worried in case she may be missing something.

'Where do we go from here?' asks Robyn, as I make my way over to my comfy leather armchair or 'thinking chair', as I like to call it, to ponder our next move.

'First, Lizzy, I need another cup of tea and a nice chocolate hobnob to help me think, while you cancel the rest of my appointments for today, Robyn. I suspect we'll be receiving another visit from Mr Mallon shortly.'

'How can you be so sure?' asks Robyn excitedly, for this is her first real encounter with a spirit that has been murdered, and she can barely contain her excitement.

'Because it will shortly be ten-thirty and I've a feeling that our mysterious Mr Mallon will still be keeping his appointment.'

'Oh my Lord, I think I'll join you in the tea and biscuits,' mutters Aunt Lizzy, as she makes her way back to the kitchen.

Robyn returns to the office to cancel my afternoon appointments while I work out our next plan of action. Once again I feel that wonderful combination of excitement and trepidation that makes life so worth living.

I realise immediately that this case is going to require all of my resources together with my psychic powers. I'll need to investigate every aspect of Mr Mallon's life both past and present if I'm to uncover his secret and ultimately release his now tortured soul from the 'middle life'. This is the place where souls go when people here on earth have experienced an unhappy, sudden or tragic death. They're unable to come to terms with the sudden departure from their life or loved ones here on earth and so are doomed to wander hopelessly in the 'middle life'. They're constantly searching for a way back into their earthly bodies and for justice or redemption. Unless they can achieve this they're doomed to become tortured spirits. Unable to return to their previous life on earth or cross over into the afterlife or Heaven, as we know it, where they can be at peace. These are the spirits who sometimes contact me through the doorway in my psychic dreams, hoping that I can help them make the transition on to the afterlife.

There is another place, which no soul wants to go and that is the 'dark life', better known as Hell. The souls that are sent here are evil doomed for all eternity, unable to seek solace or redemption. They become evil spirits. Sometimes they manage to find a way into the 'middle life' in order to avoid or delay their dreadful fate. These spirits are to be feared and only those with exceptional psychic powers will stand a chance against them. They have no conscience and only one objective: a soul for a soul. They seek a mortal soul to replace theirs and so save them from an eternity in the 'dark life'. Fortunately, in my career as an inceptor, I've only ever once had the misfortune to encounter one of these evil spirits, and it took all my psychic powers plus the help of my family secretly known as the 'RING' to defeat it. I pray and hope that I never have to come up against one again, for not even I, Charity Holmes, can be sure of the outcome when dealing with spirits from the 'dark life'.

For a moment it crosses my mind that the soul of Mr Mallon could be destined for the 'dark life', as I sensed his spirit was cold and ruthless and didn't seem to be seeking redemption. Although I did feel he was looking to undo the past, which may allow him to move on to the afterlife. Maybe the price he's paid in his death will be enough to save his soul or maybe his secret is so bad that he'll be damned for ever. The one thing I'm certain of is that I can't deal with this alone and must call upon the RING to help me.

The RING, six people bound together in love and trust sealed like a ring that can't be broken, which has no beginning and no end. This is my 'family', some who are born through blood and others through friendship, but all with love and trust in their hearts. You've already met two: Aunt Lizzy and Robyn. Now let me tell you about the other three: my husband Monty, his driver Jack and my best friend Sam.

Monty Holmes, my beloved husband who I first met eleven years ago when the police called me in to help them find a diplomat's nine-year-old daughter, who had been kidnapped and the case had gone cold. Monty works for the British Government in the Special Operations section, which is governed by the Secret Service department who specialise in sensitive cases. He's ten years older than me and born into British aristocracy, where his world is as opposite to mine as Heaven is to Hell. He towers over me, with slightly greying hair, sorrowful brown eyes, strong jaw line with a magnetic smile, well built but not muscular frame and a deep but soft voice. I fell completely and utterly in love with him the moment we met. Later when we were married (against his family's wishes), Monty said the moment I walked into the office his heart stopped. He knew that this was it. He'd found his soul mate, the one true pure love that had eluded him all his life. He instantly felt complete and knew the moment our eyes met that we would become as one. Since that meeting eleven years ago (where I did find the little girl through the spirit of her late mother), we are as one, completely devoted to each other. Monty often helps me in my investigations, using his connections in the Secret Service and likewise I help him on some of his cases using my psychic powers. Together we make a formidable team.

Jack Malone, Monty's driver, aged 45. Five feet, ten inches of pure muscle hidden under a driver's jacket. His square jaw line and rugged features mask a tender heart. Jack is ex SAS, in the Army Special Forces. He first met Monty 15 years ago when they worked together in special operations. They formed a deep bond, respect and affection for each other. When Jack had to resign from the Army due to ill health, Monty offered him the position as his driver. Although his job description says 'driver' Jack is much more than that and helps both Monty and me in our investigations, often using his old contacts in the Special Forces. He's the purest of friends and we trust him implicitly.

Sam (Samantha) Francis, aged 42. My oldest and dearest friend. A quick-witted and sometimes sharp-tongued (to her enemies) woman, with short black hair, dark, cat-like eyes, long pointed chin and hourglass figure. She was the only person at school who befriended and understood me. She protected me from the bullies who taunted me because I was different. She was born into wealth but lost it all when her father died suddenly of a heart attack

20

when she was eleven years old. The same year Ma passed over to the afterlife, which cemented that special bond between us. Sam's married twice, both times to much older men, looking for the father and security she lost as a child. Her first husband died in a car crash and left her very rich, but she loves her second husband Leo dearly. He's a High Court Judge who's almost 20 years older than she. He adores her and is very protective, spoiling her at every opportunity, which Sam wallows in. Although very different in our personalities, we love each other like sisters and speak to each other every day no matter where we are. Sam loves helping me in my investigations and has made many useful contacts through her network of rich powerful friends, and Leo's connections within the law. She's the truest and loyalist of friends.

Charity, **Monty**, **Robyn**, **Aunt Lizzy**, **Sam**, **Jack**. Six people brought together through blood, friendship, love and trust. We're as one. Each of us wears a ring made from the purest of metals, platinum, with the words 'In life and Spirit' inscribed inside. The RING forms a powerful force around us that no mortal or spirit can break.

I look at my watch. The time is 10.00 a.m. This time I'll be prepared when I meet the spirit of Mr Mallon. For if I'm to succeed in my quest for the truth I must be master of my own soul and not at the mercy of those souls trapped in spirit. Just then Aunt Lizzy returns with tea and biscuits and stands for a few moments quietly staring at me while I'm in deep thought.

'What is it, Lizzy, why are you staring?'

'Oh, my precious darling, when I see you in peaceful thought like that you remind me so much of your mother. You've her same eyes, heart and spirit and suddenly I'm transported back to when we were young, carefree and

21

so happy together. My heart wants to cry and laugh at the same time for I miss my beloved Mary. Even though I know her spirit surrounds us with love I sometimes wish for the warmth of her mortal body.'

'So do I, Lizzy,' says Robyn with a heavy sigh as she returns from the office.

'Distance lends enchantment. Words Ma often used to say to me when I felt alone as a child. Sometimes when she visits me in my psychic dreams she shows me the enchantment of the afterlife and I feel comforted and warm to see how happy she is,' I say, trying to comfort them both as the three of us sit for a few minutes munching chocolate hobnobs, drinking tea and feeling the warmth of our love for each other.

'Time is pressing and we must move quickly. I need to perform my chakras before I meet our American spirit, Mr Mallon. Once I've spoken to him we can initiate the TIE (a term we use meaning trace, investigate and eliminate) for which we'll need the help of the rest of the RING. I need you to contact Monty and Jack for me, Robyn, while you locate Sam, Lizzy.'

'Will you be OK on your own? Don't you want me here with you? Isn't it time that I started to learn how to use my psychic power?' Robyn says anxiously.

'This spirit is too strong and powerful and I'm afraid you're not ready yet. Your psychic powers are still in their infancy and he may use you to weaken me and I need to be stronger than him if I'm going to succeed,' I say tenderly, trying to protect her feelings as we finish our tea and hug each other before Aunt Lizzy and Robyn leave me to perform my chakras, while they contact the rest of the RING so that the TIE can begin.

With Aunt Lizzy and Robyn busy performing their tasks I sit back in my comfy leather chair to prepare myself for the coming of our American spirit. When I need to open up the doorway to those souls in the spirit world I must channel all my energies by opening up the deepest parts of my mind. This requires me to perform the chakras, an ancient form of meditation taught to me by Ma, involving seven energy centres within the body, which are positioned approximately along the line of the spine.

I close my eyes and focus my mind on the first, the root, centred at the base of my spine. Slowly I work my way up through the seven energies until I reach the seventh, the crown, at the top of my head. I open my mind to the universal unconscious, the all-seeing third eye, which opens the doorway to the world of spirits leading to the lost souls in the middle life.

Suddenly I feel it. My body begins to feel as if it's floating (even though I'm still seated in my chair), devoid of any weight like it's in space drifting through the universe. I breathe slowly and see my breath in the air. There's a chill in the room like that of a cold winter's day. Suddenly it becomes dark and still, except for the movement of the curtains hanging over my french windows leading to the garden. They rise up and move apart, the french doors open with such force that they nearly come apart from their hinges. I catch my breath, feel my heart beat faster and my body tenses with trepidation at what is about to come through the doors. For I instantly know that this spirit brings anger, hate and fear with it. I keep performing my chakras, because instinctively I sense that these feelings are not directed at me but are being carried as a penance within his tortured soul.

Then he appears, rising from the mist of the garden through the french doors into the cold stillness of my room. A tall shadowy silhouette. As he moves closer I can see the pain and anguish in his hollow eyes. His face has the look of a tortured soul (I've seen many); it's pale and devoid of any life, edged with guilt and sorrow, his lips dry and cracked, behind which are black broken teeth (synonymous with lost souls). He's about sixty years old and wears the coat of the 'dark life', which is made up of all his past sins and injustices against his fellow man when he was mortal. I've seen this coat before and hoped that I would never have to again. It's a heavy and painful coat to wear, which he can never take off, doomed to wear it for all eternity in the 'dark life'. It's his punishment. It's his burden. It's forever.

'We meet at last, Mr Mallon,' I say quickly, for past experience has taught me that if I can make the first communication when dealing face to face with the reincarnation of a spirit then the centre of power becomes mine. This is essential if I'm to keep my mortal soul and not be lost to the spirit world forever.

'Don't you remember me, Charity?' he says in that deep Southern American drawl, which although cold and hard, I sense has a warmth behind his words.

'Yes. I remember you now, you were at my seminar in South Carolina. It was about a year ago when I was giving a talk on psychic phenomena and was about half way through when you entered the room. I remember instantly being drawn to you as you walked in and immediately knew that we would see each other again in spirit. When I finished my talk our eyes met and without words we both knew that the connection was made.'

'I was meant to be at a business conference on the fifth floor, yet felt compelled to go to the third floor, finding myself walking into your seminar even though I had no idea who you were. Yet when our eyes met at the end of your talk, I saw that you saw my own demise. I rushed out afraid at my own fear and shock, for no one had ever been able to see into my heart and soul as you did that day. I knew then that time was running out.

24

Soon the past would be calling upon me to take what is owed from my present and leave me with a future of eternal damnation. Until that day last year I'd hidden in the darkest corners of my mind the price I'd have to pay for the power and riches that were mine here on earth. Suddenly I knew that retribution would be calling upon me from the 'dark life' to collect what was theirs. That day came yesterday at four o'clock on my sixtieth birthday.'

As he speaks, his voice changes and becomes quieter and softer with a terrible sadness about it. I know this voice so well for I've heard it so many times before when visited by the unhappy souls in the 'middle life', who are desperate to move into the light of the afterlife. I sense that he's done a terrible deed to achieve the power and riches he so desired in the mortal world and has left it too late to seek redemption.

'Why do you call upon me now? If your soul belongs to the "dark life" they'll want to collect it. You must know that I'll not help you take another soul or give you mine in exchange for yours so that you can avoid your destiny in the "dark life". Knowing this, what is it that you want from me and why will "they" not let me know your secret?'

He stares directly into my eyes where I see the hollow darkness in his. I see his soul burning in the 'dark life', feel his pain, hear his cries and know he's not looking to exchange a soul but to return the one he's stolen.

'Forty years ago when I was a young man of twenty I was visited by a spirit who called himself the Enchanter. He showed me the power and riches that could be mine. At first I thought it was a dream. But over a period of weeks the dream became stronger and stronger until it was real. It always occurred around four o'clock in the morning when I would wake up unable to go back to sleep. This spirit was incredibly handsome, strong and powerful. He seemed to know me, my desires, my dreams,

25

my inner thoughts. He knew that I'd left my past behind and was seeking a new beginning and offered me all that I desired plus more. I began to look forward to his visits, where he'd show me the enchantment of my new life. Then suddenly he stopped coming and for weeks I couldn't eat or sleep. All I wanted was for him to return. Then it happened.'

He paused for a moment, his eyes etched with pain, his voice weak and afraid, his hands and body shaking with fear and shame. I knew then that he'd given his soul to the Enchanter in return for power and riches. But the Enchanter doesn't give an eternity of happiness, he simply promises you all your desires and it takes a very strong mortal to resist him. He knows this and so visits those whose desires are stronger than their will to see beyond the enchantment. This spirit is evil and comes in all manner of disguises, male or female. He appears to offer all that you desire and hope for but never shows you the ultimate price that you'll have to pay, that the coat you wear for all eternity is that of the 'dark life', and not the sumptuous one that he comes visiting in.

'You gave him your soul, but needed another one to replace it,' I said, both angry and sad at the same time. For although I knew he had done a terrible thing, I also knew that it would take a very strong and special person to resist the Enchanter.

He looked down to hide his eyes from mine and for a moment I felt his sorrow and despair at what he'd done. Then he raised his head slowly with tears of blood flowing from his eyes and said, 'It's a terrible thing that I've done and I don't seek your forgiveness or understanding, because until our paths crossed last year I felt no shame or regret. I revelled in the power and riches that had become mine and gave no thought to the soul that I stole to attain them. I've been ruthless and devoid of any

26

human warmth to my fellow human beings, destroying many a life along the way without conscience. My family despise me and there's only ever been one true love in my mortal life. Now I have to pay a terrible price for my desires. I have just twenty-eight days to find the body of the man whose soul I stole and give it back. If I fail then at ten-thirty in the morning, twenty-eight days from now the Enchanter will come to collect and I will be dammed for all eternity in the "dark life".'

'Why have you been given twenty-eight days? The Enchanter isn't of a generous nature and always collects what is due to him.' I ask, intrigued, as I've never known a soul destined to be a spirit in the 'dark life' to be given a second chance.

'My death was premature as I was murdered twenty-eight days before the Enchanter was due to collect. He can't collect until the contract date, which was when I stole the soul forty years ago on the first of June. The soul of a man who died at six that same day.'

Now I see the connection of the times, which I had felt so strongly before, the visits at 4.00 a.m. by the Enchanter and the death of the man whose soul was stolen to replace his at 6.00 a.m. The subsequent reincarnation of this soul at 10.30 a.m., who then became Mr Mallon. But there are still so many other questions that our American spirit needs to answer! Why and who murdered Mr Mallon this morning? Was it just a coincidence that it was the same time as the visits he received from the Enchanter 40 years ago? Who is Mr Mallon? For in order to swap souls both mortals have to die. The one who has signed the contract with the Enchanter (in this instance Mr Mallon) takes the other soul, leaving his soul with the Enchanter, ready for collection on the contract date. The spirit of the man whose soul was stolen remains without peace, doomed to wander hopelessly in the darkness unable to cross over into the 'middle' or afterlife. It's a terrible fate. The Enchanter always collects and never relinquishes a soul. He's the Anti-Angel. He's Lucifer. He's the Devil. He's Evil personified.

'Who were you before you swapped souls? Who murdered you this morning and why? Is the murderer connected to the Enchanter? If so why would he collect his dues twenty-eight days early? Why not search for the body of the man whose soul you stole and return it yourself? For you must know that while you are in the "middle life" your powers are strong and you could search in the world of darkness and find him. You can seek justice and redemption yourself for you still have twenty-eight days. Why do you call upon me? What is it that I can do that you can't?'

He moves closer towards me and I feel the coldness of his body as he leans down to look deep into my eyes. It's then that I understand.

'Because of the wickedness of my sins the great Prophet Ezekiel – now one of God's trusted archangels – has been sent to the "middle life". He's told me that it would be too easy to use my powers. I have to prove that I'm truly repentant of my crimes against humanity and worthy to be saved from an eternity in the "dark life". Therefore I can't seek justice and redemption for myself. Ezekiel has allowed me to seek you out and ask for your help. But like a riddle that needs to be unravelled I can't give you the answers only clues in the hope that you can save my soul from eternal damnation before ten-thirty on the first of June. You must discover my secret yourself.'

Then he raises his head, stands erect and proud, looking deep into my eyes and pleads. 'Charity Holmes, I charge you to save my soul and to seek justice for my murderer and redemption for my sins. Do you accept this quest?'

I look straight into his pale face and feel the pain and

28

sorrow within his soul and know that I can't refuse. Accepting this quest means I will save his soul, but also the one that he stole, as well as seeking justice for his murderer. I stand erect and reply. 'I accept.'

Instantly I see a light within his eyes. He looks directly at me, smiles gently as he disappears back through the french doors into the mist from whence he came. I feel a sense of excitement and wonder at the challenge ahead of me, but know that time is of the essence and the price that'll be paid if I fail. The burden of responsibility never weighed as heavy on my shoulders as it does at this moment. I can't. I shan't. I won't fail.

3

Divine Guidance

The darkness and cold lift from the room and the brightest of lights suddenly shines through the french doors onto my face. It's the most magical of moments as I feel its warmth, love and protection. I know instantly that it's no ordinary light. I've seen and felt it before, when my beloved Ma visits me during the night in my psychic dreams. It's the light of the afterlife. It's the light of the 'One True Being'. It's the light of God. I close my eyes and bask in this glorious mystical light and feel the love and power of God upon me.

Then I hear her voice. 'My darling daughter.'

I open my eyes and see her floating before me. The most beautiful of visions – a pure white translucent light, with her magnificent long flowing hair and the purest of smiles emanating from her gentle face.

'Ma,' I say with tears in my eyes, for my heart is both bursting with joy and broken with sadness at the same time. Joy for seeing her again and sadness that she is not of mortal flesh and blood. Suddenly I realise that it's the first time she's materialised to me during the day. It has always been at night in my psychic dreams, when she brings me comfort and love to soothe my troubled mind. It's in the early hours of the morning that I'm most vulnerable to the spirit world, as sometimes my dreams can be both dangerous and traumatic. Ma knows this and often comes to me at night after I've had one of my dreams to help me sleep.

'Charity, my sweet beautiful child, I've been sent to tell you that you're being divinely guided and it's imperative, now more than ever, that you trust your gift. The knowingness, the visions, the inner voice, they're all showing you the way to the truth. Don't be swayed and led into another path, for evil is all around you and is waiting.'

'Who sent you, Ma? What evil? Who is it that I should fear?'

Ma floats towards me, stretching out her soft white hands to cup my face in her palms as she looks deep into my eyes where I see ... a young boy aged about 15 years, who is tall and gangly with dark hair, a pale complexion and deep black eyes playing by a stream. He looks innocent and happy. He's simple and trusting of mind but has a true heart. He looks up for a moment. I look into his soul and see darkness, pain and sorrow. I hear his cries. He disappears into the mist that surrounds him. Suddenly I feel cold and fearful. My blood chills and my hands shake. My throat is tight and my heart is beating out of control. I start to breathe faster and faster and feel a terrible sense of darkness and despair. I close my eyes.

'Ma, Ma please stop, I don't want to see any more,' I cry, for I know what she's about to show me is not warm and loving but cold and dark. Ma has never shown me dark visions before and for the first time I'm afraid to look deeper in to the all-seeing third eye.

'Don't be afraid, my darling. Trust me. You must look. Whatever you see will be your divine guidance. It'll lead you to the truth.'

I open my eyes and what I see is the darkest of visions

as the room goes black. I can still feel Ma's hands holding my face, knowing that she's protecting me and that I won't come to any harm, but still I can't stop my fear as the room fills with the sound of souls crying in anguish and despair. They float above and around me, shadowy dark figures that are translucent in appearance but dim like a fading light. Then they appear from within the darkness, shadowy silhouettes that have no faces. When I have one of my psychic dreams or visions the messages within them are often complex and hard to unravel, but if I look deep enough and follow my intuition and use my gift then eventually I'll see the truth. At first the silhouettes appear handsome and strong, but as they draw closer I realise they're dark and evil and to be feared. There are three of them: two men and a woman who are faceless yet I can see their true souls. The man and woman who walk together I sense are young, but their hearts are cold and hard, showing that they live only for themselves. Instantly my gift tells me that they're not yet of the spirit world. The other man, who walks alone in the centre of the two, completely encircled by a ring of fire, is immensely powerful and strong. I feel his illimitable hate. His silhouette is that of a handsome man but his true soul is the ugliest of creatures; it's the beast that lurks within us all, which can be woken at any time. The souls that float around them, even though they're evil and deserve their pain, I sense are afraid of the handsome one in the middle. The three can't speak, but I know they don't want to be in my vision; they are there against their will. They're fighting to leave and soon they win the battle and are gone, for the power that sent them can't hold them for long. The room remains black with the fading souls still crying and floating in despair.

Two more shadowy figures float out of the mist into the room. One is a tall man wearing a heavy dark coat; the other a young woman. They walk together holding hands. Again they've no features and are just silhouettes. The souls floating above move closer to taunt them with their cries of pain and anguish. They don't fear them like the first three silhouettes and enjoy making them feel the torture of eternal darkness. I look closer and although I see no faces I immediately know that the tall man is Stephen Mallon. I don't know the woman but feel her love for him and her anguish, fear and pain. She's not of spirit yet nor is her soul evil. They look at me but are unable to speak for they are but a vision in a dream sent to me by divine guidance. Like the other three souls they're here not out of choice, but because the power that sent them is more powerful than they are.

Suddenly the room is lifted from blackness and I'm back in the warmth and luminous light of Ma's love and protection and my heart is light again. I breathe softly and have no fear as her hands are still lovingly cupped around my face. All the dark souls are gone and my quiet room is once again my safe haven. I look into Ma's beautiful face and say, 'I know that you've been sent by God, but why? What is it about Stephen Mallon that he wants to show me? Why does he want to save the soul of a man who has done the darkest of deeds and stolen another man's soul?'

Ma lifts her hands and floats upwards into the middle of the room, looking down on me, her translucent light glowing brighter and brighter. I feel her love and warmth. She raises her right hand and blows me a kiss (just as she always did when I was a child and we were to be parted) saying softly, 'Follow the vision and you'll know the truth. Remember, even the good fall from grace. God always protects the good and fights the evil. Search for the good to destroy the evil. Always remember I'm with you. You're not alone.'

With those words I watch Ma gently float away and I'm left to ponder on yet more riddles upon riddles, but there's one thing that I know to be true. Stephen Mallon has a soul that is deserving of God's divine intervention. Once again I ask myself, Who is Stephen Mallon? Where did he come from? Was he murdered as a punishment for his sins or to save his soul from the Enchanter?

I sink back in my chair knowing that in 28 days time if I've not uncovered the truth, then his soul will be lost forever.

4

The Dark One

After opening my mind to the universal unconscious by performing the chakras and entering the world of spirits I now need to close down or un-tune from the collective unconscious. Otherwise I'll experience disharmony within my 'energetic bodies'. As an inceptor I must be responsible not only for my mind, body and spirit, but also for those around me. I must close down after using my all-seeing third eye otherwise the deepest parts of my mind will still be open to the doorway leading to the 'middle life', where the souls and spirits there can still enter. As before, when performing the chakras to open my mind, I must now perform it again to close the doorway. If I don't do this I'm unable to live in the mortal world in peace. I will be open to dreams and visions from the spirit world continuously and at their mercy. It's only through many years of learning and knowledge that I'm able to open and close my mind to the world of spirits at my will and not theirs. It has given me the peace that I didn't have as a child, when I felt frightened and alone, unable to understand or control what was happening to me. The chakras are only one of the many tools that I now use to channel and control my psychic powers to enable me to fulfil my destiny as the Inceptor. I close my eyes to perform the seven energies of the chakras, working backwards. I stand erect from my chair, raising my arms high above my head, stretching my body, knowing that now I'm ready to begin my quest when the door opens.

'Well, what happened? Did you see him? What did he say? Tell us everything,' Robyn asks, excited like a teenager on her first date, as she enters the room with Aunt Lizzy trailing behind her.

'Give her a chance will yah now, for you know how tiring it is visiting the spirit world, Robyn, darling,' Aunt Lizzy says quickly in her protective motherly voice.

'Now, now, you two, settle down,' I say, smiling to myself as the two of them banter away together. 'Before I relay details, what's happening with the rest of the RING? Have you contacted Monty and Jack, Robyn, and what about Sam, Lizzy?'

'Yes. Yes. And yes,' they both reply quickly while making their way to the couch, where they proceed to make themselves comfortable ready for my usual 'blow by blow' account, for they love listening to me report on my 'psychic moments', as Monty loves to describe them. Robyn pipes in first, eager to get down to business. For in her mind she's not just a secretary but the next Charity Holmes, inceptor extraordinaire. It's comforting to know that I'll be passing the mantle to her one day, when she'll become a great inceptor. But not yet, for I still have many quests ahead of me.

'Monty and Jack are coming up tomorrow morning from home. They're just tidying up some loose ends from the "Poleaxe" case. I've appraised them of the situation and Monty's checking the background of Mr Mallon through his usual connections and hopes to have some info for us later today. He'll try and ring you tonight but is in debriefing most of the day and night so it might be very late. Jack knows someone in forensics at Scotland Yard and has arranged to meet them later on today to see what more he can dig up about the actual murder. I'm thinking of giving Sergeant Dredge a bell and working the old magic on him to see what I can turn up.'

'Well done. As usual, Robyn, you're ahead of me, and Sergeant Dredge looks like a man that could do with a little "light" in his life,' I say with a large smile on my face for I know only too well the string of broken hearts Robyn leaves in her trail. But one day she'll meet her soul mate and then what a team they'll be. Formidable just like Monty and me!

Aunt Lizzy jumps in to report that her task is duly completed as well. 'After an enormous amount of searching and phone calls I managed to locate Sam. She's in New York attending some fancy ladies' convention of all things and won't be back for another couple of days. But when I told her about the American spirit that was it, she was on the case. Already she's talking about checking him out through her connections in America and says she'll ring you as soon as she's anything concrete.'

'Oh how I love it when the RING are together,' I say as the three of us clench our right hands firmly to form a fist while stretching our arms out to meet in a circle, to enable our rings to cement together as one. We often perform this little ceremony when we're about to embark on a new quest together to seal our love and trust in each other. I then proceed to tell the story of my visions. Robyn and Aunt Lizzy listen quietly as it slowly dawns on them how dangerous and treacherous our journey for the truth will be and the dark, evil forces we're up against.

'Well now you know what I know,' I say quietly, although secretly I'm afraid at what dark forces we'll come against in our quest for the American spirit.

Robyn and Aunt Lizzy turn and look at each other knowing that we can't turn back now whatever our fears. For the spirits have spoken and when that happens we have no choice but to accede to their will if we are to win the battle against evil.

'What's next then?' Robyn asks thoughtfully and slightly more subdued than when she first entered the room.

'Firstly I need to visit the Dorchester Hotel and see the room where Mallon was murdered. For I'm sure once I'm there I'll be able to connect – feel his and his murderer's presence in the room – then I can pick up the trail that'll lead us to the next clue. Next stop will be the mortuary to see his body, where I shall use my psychic powers to get closer to him.'

'I want to come with you to the hotel and mortuary. I know that my gift isn't as powerful as yours but I'm sure that I can be of help to you. Please don't say no for I really need to do this. I need to learn how to use and channel my gift. If you keep trying to protect me from the evil spirits I'll never become as good an inceptor as you. You must allow me to enter the dark side of the spirit world as well as the light. Please let me help you, Charity. Let me do this with you,' Robyn pleads, anxious to prove herself.

I listen quietly, realising that she's right. I love her so much that I want to protect her from all that is evil both in the mortal and spirit world, but I must allow her to know the dark side if she's going to be able to use her psychic powers to their fullest potential when fighting evil. 'OK, Robyn, we'll do this journey together for the 'visions' have shown me that we are fighting the darkest of evils and both our powers will be needed to succeed.'

'Great, I'll put Sergeant Dredge on hold until tomorrow,' Robyn replies, excited and fearless at the same time. For her experience of souls from the spirit world has been limited so far and I'm afraid she's in for an awakening like no other.

'What about me? What's my task? I don't want to be

38

left here while you two are off enjoying yourselves,' Aunt Lizzy scowls in her sulky 'I'm in the RING too' Irish brogue.

'It's vital that we know as much as possible about the Mallon family. I know that Monty, Jack and Sam are checking them out but I suspect that he's probably stayed at the Dorchester Hotel before. So I need you to use your Irish charm on the staff there while Robyn and I are in his room. They must have a record somewhere in their files of when he or his family stayed there before. For if my suspicions are correct, whoever murdered him knew their way around the hotel and how to get into his room at four o'clock in the morning. Also, it's clear to me from the messages in my visions that he knew his murderer. He may even have been expecting him or her for I suspect when we check his room out we'll find that there was no forced entry. Mallon himself either let in the murderer or they had a key. If the latter is the case how and where did they get the key from?'

'What makes you think he knew his murderer?' asks Aunt Lizzy, as she sits up straight, preening herself like a fine-feathered peacock, full of self-importance now that she's an integral part of the team and has been given the go ahead to nose around the hotel. For if there is one thing Aunt Lizzy loves more than food it's digging in to people's pasts and finding all sorts of skeletons.

'Mallon was murdered twenty-eight days before his soul was due to be taken by the Enchanter. This is the key to everything. Someone knew that he was due to die. The question is who would gain the most if he were killed before the first of June? Was he killed for greed, hate or love? If he was killed for greed then I suspect it was a member of his own family, but which family, as in my visions I see more than one. There is the young man and woman who walk together with the handsome man,

39

who I believe to be the Enchanter, all of whom possess the darkest of souls. But only the silhouette in the middle is in spirit. The other two are still mortal, yet there's something malevolent about them. My gift of "clear seeing" tells me that it's pure evil, but I've yet to uncover where or how this evil has manifested itself in what I fear we'll discover are Mallon's children. Should it be for hate then it could be someone from either his past or present, who, through his ruthless and cold-blooded ambition, has been destroyed in some way. There's the young boy aged about fifteen who in my vision was once happy and pure of heart, playing by a stream and who is suddenly lost and in darkness. My gift shows me that he's from the past and yet somehow I feel he's still in the present. Did he come back to kill Mallon? Or was it someone in the present – a business associate who would gain from his death? Or was he killed for love? In my other vision I see him walking hand in hand with a young woman whose soul, like the other two, is still mortal yet her heart is pure, but she's paid a high price for loving Mallon, as I see she's destined for the 'dark life'. She is, I suspect, his 'other family'. In his first vision he told me that he had 'only ever loved once' in his mortal life. She is, I believe, the result of that love. All of the above knew Mallon and all have reasons to see him dead before the first of June. But I suspect the Enchanter is not one of them.'

Robyn and Aunt Lizzy, who've been listening intently, ask, 'But the Enchanter wants his soul, therefore he would want him dead in order to collect?'

'But not until the contract date, which is twenty-eight days from now. Mallon told me that Ezekiel, one of God's archangels, has given him the opportunity to prove that his soul is worth saving from the Enchanter. God has, by divine intervention through Ma's materialisation, shown me that Mallon is not all evil and is worth saving. Therefore I don't think he was murdered by the Enchanter but by someone else whose reasons meant that he had to die before the contract date. Again the question is, was he murdered for greed, hate or love and by someone from the past, present or future?'

The three of us once again stand silently for a few moments, for the more we look into the reasons for his murder the more questions we seem to uncover. Then Robyn asks thoughtfully, 'How are we going to get into the room? The staff won't let us in without good reason. Also I suspect that the room has been sealed by the police with a guard at the door until they've finished all their investigations.'

'I'm Mallon's personal psychic adviser whose appointment was not kept due to his murder. They're not to know that we've never met before except for our brief encounter last year, so we'll use that as leverage to gain entry into his room. We have the record of the telephone call from his room to my office this morning and your subsequent telephone call with the receptionist as proof of connection. That I think will be enough to whet their curiosity. With my psychic powers, you working your *femme fatale* prowess on the police guard outside the door and Lizzy's Irish charm it's a cinch.' I check my watch – the time is twelve noon. 'We'd better get going if we're to get to the hotel and mortuary before the end of the day, and while we still have the light of day on our side.'

We arrive at the Dorchester Hotel around 12.45 p.m. taking in its regal beauty and opulent surroundings. Clearly with its grand entrance and nouveau riche style only the very wealthy can afford to stay here. We begin our investigation as Lizzy heads straight for the reception desk with her Irish charm in full flow, while Robyn and I make our way to the hotel room. It's not difficult to find, as Robyn had already got his room number from the receptionist when she spoke to her on the telephone this morning. We arrive on the third floor and immediately see our first obstacle, namely one very bored-looking police constable guarding room 36. It's time for Robyn to work her charm while I play the 'dotty psychic'. It can sometimes be fortuitous to ham it up a bit. I tend to find that if you give a performance to the right audience (in this instance a bored and not too bright-looking police constable) a lot can be achieved.

'Oh, this must be the room, my dear, perhaps this very nice policeman can assist us,' I say to Robyn as we make our way towards the room.

Immediately the police constable wakes from his bored slumber and instantly starts checking Robyn out, with that slow all over body glance that men do when that old animal lust rears its head. Robyn instantly moves into action. Sliding coyly but ever so seductively towards the police constable, she says, 'Can you help us, Constable? Miss Holmes had an appointment with her client Mr Stephen Mallon this morning. Unfortunately it was meant to be with his mortal body but instead ended up talking to his spirit. She's a psychic investigator, you see. Miss Holmes needs to connect more closely with her client in order to assist the police with his murder investigation.'

The police constable smiles, somewhat bemused at what he's just heard, and yet cannot help feeling somewhat drawn to the delightfully pretty, if somewhat scatty, young thing in front of him.

'Well, I can't let you in I'm afraid. It's a crime scene and official police officers allowed in only,' he replies, smirking at me but smiling sweetly at Robyn.

'Oh, my. Oh, my, Chief Inspector Cranky won't be too

42

pleased to hear that I've been treated in this manner, especially as I'm such an integral part of his investigative team,' I say in a rather dotty but somehow 'you'll be sorry if you don't let me in' tone.

Then Robyn flashes her *femme fatale* smile directly at the police constable, saying, 'Oh dear, you look such a nice policeman that I wouldn't want you to get in to any trouble, but I'm sure when we report back to the Chief Inspector that we've had a wasted journey he won't be too happy. He's not the most sensitive of creatures.'

The police constable looks a little more worried now, because he has heard of Chief Inspector Cranky and his rather unforgiving nature.

'Well you both look harmless enough and if you are very quick and quiet then I don't see that a few minutes will make much difference. I mean, how long do you need to "connect" with the victim?' he says with a big grin on his face.

'We're very old friends, Constable, so I'm sure I will be receiving messages fairly quickly,' I reply as the two of us speedily make our way into the room.

We enter the room, or more aptly, suite, for once inside it's more like an apartment. We begin by looking around the large reception room with fitted bar, small kitchen and large windows overlooking the front of the hotel. I feel nothing and know instantly that this room is free of any presence as I look at Robyn and sense that she feels the same. We make our way to the bedroom with its large king-sized bed in the middle of the room, walk-in wardrobes on the right and marble *en suite* bathroom to the left. It's a bright room with the sun shinning through the huge french windows onto the bed where we see the silhouette. The police have drawn the outline of Mallon's body on the bed sheets. The silhouette indicates that he was lying on his back with his head slightly turned to the left and his arms and legs stretched out. There are four marks showing where the stab wounds were, one on the middle of his forehead, one on his chest and one either side of his breasts. Immediately I see that if you link them up they make the sign of the cross. There's blood all over the sheets and pillowcases with splashes on the headboard, wall and floor where there are footprints in the blood. I look more closely to see that there is more than one set of footprints.

'Hmm, that's interesting, Robyn, it looks to me as if there are two or more different footprints. What do you think?'

There's no response from Robyn so I look up to see her standing by the bed transfixed by the silhouette and all the blood surrounding it. 'It's not a pretty sight, I'm afraid. Are you OK to carry on?' I ask.

'Yes, I'm fine. It's just that I've never seen so much blood before. Why would someone want to kill a man in this way? Look at the stab wounds – they seem to form the sign of the cross. It's almost as if it was a ritual.'

'That's because it's a ritual death,' I reply. 'He's been murdered in this way for a particular reason and the sign of the cross is very relevant. Look at the way his body is laid out.'

'I'm not sure what you mean? What's unusual about how he's lying?' asks Robyn, puzzled and staring more intensely at the figure drawn on the sheets.

'Most people don't sleep stretched out in that way. It would be very uncomfortable. I would say that he was awake and knew his killer or killers and did nothing to prevent them stabbing him. It's almost as if he was pre-pared to die and just lay there waiting for the inevitable.'

'Do you mean he was expecting his killers and let them in? Or they let themselves in and he wasn't surprised to see them in his bedroom and just did nothing?'

'I would say that's a fair assumption, Robyn. Did you notice that the door was intact when we entered the room, which confirms my suspicions that there was no forced entry. Therefore it's clear to me that the killer or killers either let themselves in or were let in by Mallon himself. Also take a look at the footprints on the bloodstained floor by the bed and tell me what you make of them.'

Robyn moves around to where I'm standing, which is on the left hand side of the bed near the french windows where we both bend down to take a closer look at the footprints.

'Well there's definitely more than one set of footprints. I'm no expert but would say that there were three, one large and two smaller ones,' Robyn says, looking intrigued.

We both follow the footprints. Two almost together, one large – approximately size nine – male shoe, and one smaller – size six female shoe with a heel. Although we can see the footprints, they're faint. The other footprint is very tiny, probably a size three or four with a flatter heel, but again definitely female, and is much more prominent and completely separate from the other two. They lead from the side of the bed through the bedroom into the reception room and finally disappear at the door.

'I think that we have two separate sets of footprints. One is almost certainly the killer and the other two have come in later and found the body.'

'How do you come to that conclusion?' asks Robyn, who by now is completely enthralled by the crime scene in front of her.

'The first footprint is much deeper, and as you can see, quite separate from the other two, which indicates to me firstly that the blood was still fresh and therefore was probably made by the killer. Which we can probably safely surmise is a woman who is petite in size and I

45

would say entered and left separately to the other two. They came along later as the footprints are much fainter, which means the blood was dried into the carpet. I would say they arrived at least one, maybe two hours after Mallon was murdered and before the porter arrived at six. This would make the time between five and five-thirty. What we don't know is whether the killer let herself in with a key or was let in by Mallon or perhaps found the door unlocked and simply opened it. The other two who followed later I would say probably had a key, as I'm fairly sure that the killer wouldn't leave the door opened or unlocked.'

Robyn stares admiringly, saying, 'All that from three sets of footprints. Now I know why you have such an awesome reputation. Not much gets past you.'

'Thanks, my dear. I like to keep the brain cells fully operational and there's nothing like a good crime scene to test them.'

After standing for a few moments in the reception room congratulating ourselves on our sharp detective skills, we then make our way back into the bedroom. For Robyn and I now need to channel our energies in the hope that we might be able to gain some more clues as to who were the three people in the bedroom when Mallon was murdered. It won't be easy, for there have been many other mortal souls in and out of this room since the murder. Once back in the bedroom I look around for a significator (something personal belonging to Mallon), which we can use to form a connection with him. Robyn looks in the bathroom while I look around the bed and in the wardrobe. I'm beginning to feel despondent as the room has been cleared of all personal effects by either the police or his family. Then suddenly I spot something shimmering behind the bedside cabinet and bend down to look closer. It's a gold cufflink. I shout to Robyn excitedly, 'I have found the significator, we can begin.'

As Robyn rushes back into the bedroom I look at her for a moment and then ask, 'Are you ready and prepared for what may happen once we connect with the significator?'

'I am,' she replies, swiftly, with that steely confidence in her voice.

We both make our way back into the reception room where I take out my black velvet casting cloth from my bag, which I use to place the cufflink on. We place both the cloth with the cufflink on top of it on the coffee table and then sit close. We take our right hands and place them together over the cufflink and then close our eyes. Slowly we repeat within our 'inner voice' the chakras, in order to clear our minds so that the doorway to the spirit world is open. Then suddenly we can feel the presence.

Instantly we both let go of the cufflink, for immediately we sense that it's evil. The room descends into a blackness that I've never felt or seen before. Robyn grabs my arm and looks despairingly at me, her eyes transfixed with fear. I squeeze her hand firmly looking deep into her now terrified face and say calmly, 'Whatever you see, don't let them into your soul. Keep concentrating on your chakras. Repeat it over and over again so that your body, mind, soul and spirit are as one and untouchable by any evil that would want to enter. Let me do the talking. Just concentrate and give me your strength and together we'll conquer this dark spirit.'

The room fills with dark, shadowy translucent souls who are floating above and around us, taunting us with their shrieks of pain and despair. Some are laughing, others crying as they swoop down and enter in and out of our bodies, trying to find the beast that is within us all to corrupt and claim our souls. I hold on tightly to

47

Robyn and whisper to her, 'Be strong, don't let them in. Close your mind and heart to them and think only of love and goodness. Remember the RING. Hold onto that and they won't be able to enter.'

Just at that moment the door opens and in enters the police constable guarding the room. 'I heard noises ... what the hell is going on here?' he shouts, by now completely transfixed in the middle of the room as the dark souls swoop towards him eager to enter into his mortal body to steal his goodness and awaken the beast within.

'Close your eyes. Don't look at them,' I shout. 'They mustn't enter your body. Think only of a loved one or song that makes you feel happy and secure, then keep repeating that loved one's name or song over and over again in your mind. Don't let them enter your thoughts. You mustn't look at them, and keep your mind and thoughts pure so that they can't get inside you. Listen to me and you'll be safe.'

Suddenly the cufflink rises up from the black velvet casting cloth and begins to spin in the air, growing bigger and bigger, forming a huge open void of fire in front of us. It appears three-dimensional, as deep and endless as space itself but within the fire is the blackest of holes, which mesmerizes us as the souls floating around whisper and call to us to enter it. I feel my heart beating so fast that I fear it will burst as I'm rooted to the spot unable to move as sheer terror spreads over my body. For I know what manner of monster is about to manifest itself from this void of evil that now tries to encompass us. I try to speak to Robyn but have no voice. My mind starts racing and my breathing becomes fast and erratic as I feel the panic racing through my blood. I dig deep into the pit of my soul to concentrate my mind and slowly remember who I am and the power of my gift, which will see me through.

I begin to breathe slowly and feel my heartbeat gradually slow down. I open my mouth and the words start to form. 'Whatever comes through that void, don't look into its eyes, don't speak to it and remember to keep your mind and thoughts pure. For whatever the vision, remember, it's not mortal. It's not spirit. It's Beelzebub. It's the Antichrist. It's Lucifer. It's the Devil.'

I turn and look at Robyn and stretch my hand out to hold hers as we fix our eyes on each other and smile knowing that as long as we remain as one and focus our gift to form a shield against the 'Dark One' then we shan't come to any harm. I quickly look back at the police constable who stands like stone with his eyes closed constantly repeating the words 'Louise, my love' over and over to himself. I shout, 'Remain as you are. Don't open you eyes and keep repeating your words. Wait for my signal and you'll be safe.'

Then it appears...

From within the void of fire it glides towards us, growing bigger and bigger until the whole room is engulfed in its presence. The darkest of creatures with its eyes burning with evil desire yet it has no face, for should we look into its eyes we would see our own reflection. For the Devil's face is that of pure evil. It's the beast that lurks within us all. Look into the soul of the 'Dark One' and he'll steal yours. He'll awaken all your darkest thoughts and desires and you'll become his, as black and perilous as the thick fluid that immerses itself in everything it touches, which tries to swallow you up into its jaws. All the evil souls in the room rush into the darkness and I hear their cries of pain and anguish, and although I know they deserve their fate, I can't help but feel pity for they are lost eternally to the 'dark life'.

Then it speaks… The most demonic of voices I have ever heard.

'Charity, oh thou ever so sweet Charity, do you really think that your pitiful gift will be strong enough to fight me? What's mine is mine and won't be taken from me. I will collect. You can't defeat me. Your god is weak. I'm the "True One".'

Suddenly the void of fire returns to nothingness, taking all the lost souls with it as the cufflink falls to the floor and once again peace and light return to the room. I feel a sharp pain in my hand and look down to see it has turned blue where Robyn and I have held onto each other so tight. We continue to hold each other tightly until we finally feel safe and our bodies slowly stop shaking, knowing that it was our gift and the love and trust in each other that kept us from the jaws of Hell. As I bend down to pick up the cufflink from the floor I now know that it doesn't belong to Mallon, but was left by a much darker and more evil person whose footprints are indelibly etched in his blood on the bedroom floor. This I fear is no ordinary man for he has the protection of the Devil himself.

'What an evil man Mallon must have been to bring forth the Lord of Darkness,' says Robyn, somewhat shaken but proud of herself at the same time for surviving the darkest of moments.

'This wasn't Mallon's cufflink,' I say as I put it in my bag. 'I suspect it belongs to the man who left the other footprint, and when we find the other cufflink we find him. Well I think we are done here. Let's go and see what Lizzy has uncovered.' As we turn to make our way towards the door we see the police constable still standing there frozen to the spot with his eyes closed mumbling away. We can't help giggling, thinking to ourselves that it's just as well we have our own powers to draw upon, otherwise we'd certainly not be walking out of this room today.

'You can open your eyes now, Constable, for all the monsters are gone,' I say with a big grin on my face. After all, he did say we were harmless! Then we both thank him and quickly rush out of the room, leaving him standing there totally bemused and bewildered. Back down by the reception desk we catch up with Lizzy, who's looking very pleased with herself.

'Did yah discover anything, girls?' she asks as we make our way back to the car.

I quickly put Lizzy in the picture. 'Well we know that there were three people, two women and a man in Mallon's room on the morning of his murder. One woman came in earlier and was probably the killer and the other two followed later, the reasons why we've yet to discover. We have a cufflink that was left behind, which we're fairly certain belongs to the other man and not Mallon.'

As Robyn drives us to the mortuary, Lizzy gives her report.

'Well, Charity, my darling, when I told the receptionist and assistant manager who you were and about the phone call from Mallon they couldn't have been more helpful. While I was having some delicious cake and tea they checked their records and you were right, he'd stayed there before on several occasions. Mostly he booked in alone on business trips but sometimes his wife would join him later. They always had the same suite – number thirty-six. His wife didn't join him this time but did ring him from America just before he went into the restaurant at seven o'clock on the evening of his arrival. After he finished his meal he had a drink at the bar and then went to the reception desk to request an early morning call for six finally retiring to his room at ten, stating that he didn't want to be disturbed. At about eleven a man

51

and woman arrived and signed in as Alex and Lucy Mallon, claiming to be his children. They enquired what room he was in but said they wouldn't disturb him so late at night and would meet up at breakfast. The porter helped them with their luggage to room forty-eight, which is on the floor above Mallon's. When his body was discovered at six the police interviewed them at approximately seven. They subsequently requested a line to call their mother in America at around seven-forty-five. The hotel has reserved a room for Mrs Mallon and is expecting her to arrive later on this evening.'

'Excellent, Lizzy, now we know the identity of the other two footprints, his son and daughter. It would be simple to gain access to his room once they were staying in the hotel, especially as he always stays in the same room, number thirty-six. It would also be very easy to get a spare key cut by a member of staff who wasn't averse to earning a little extra money.'

'What about the cufflink? Do you think it belongs to the son? What about the other woman, his killer? How did she gain access the room?' asks Robyn as we arrive at the mortuary.

'I fear the cufflink does belong to the son, who I'm now positive is the one who has the protection of the Devil, and we must be very careful when dealing with him. The other woman is still a mystery.'

We enter the mortuary and make our way to the attendant on the desk, contemplating on how we're going to get past him to view the body. Fortunately for us the man on the desk knows who I am. He's a nervous little man aged about thirty-five with an irritating habit of sniffing continuously.

'Oh, Miss Holmes, this is an honour (sniff, sniff) I'm a great fan of yours (sniff, sniff). I have attended many of your talks and seminars on psychic phenomena and mediumship (sniff, sniff) for I've the gift myself you know (sniff, sniff).'

'Well you're certainly in the right place to use your gift Mr, er...'

'Call me Andy, Miss Holmes (sniff, sniff) no need for formalities between us psychics (sniff, sniff).'

'Thank you, Andy, and what a pleasure to meet a fellow kindred spirit for we require your help,' I say, appealing to his ego.

'Ah so you're on a case (sniff, sniff)? Anything I can do to help just ask (sniff, sniff)!'

'My colleagues and I are investigating the murder of a Mr Stephen Mallon, an American whose body I believe you have here?'

His eyes light up and his whole body starts twitching with the excitement of being actually involved in one of Charity Holmes, the famous psychic investigator's cases.

'Indeed, Miss Holmes, he was brought in at ten-thirty this morning (sniff, sniff). Officially I shouldn't let you see the body unless you're a relative or police (sniff, sniff), but I'm sure it'll be OK in this instance (sniff, sniff).'

Again Robyn, Lizzy and I look at each other, for the time of 10.30 a.m. keeps cropping up. The appointment made by Robyn for Mallon at 10.30 a.m. The man whose body he entered 40 years ago to steal his soul at 10.30 a.m. on 1st June, and the collection date in 28 days time by the Enchanter at 10.30 a.m. Now his body arrives at the mortuary at precisely 10.30 a.m.

We follow Andy to the refrigeration units where he pulls out Mallon's body and removes the sheet covering him. At last we see the mortal body of our American spirit and I know instantly that he's the man in my visions – the tall man, aged about 60 years, with hollow, jet-black eyes and pale, lifeless face etched with pain and sorrow, who materialised before me in my quiet room; the shadowy, faceless silhouette holding the young woman's hand sent to me by God's divine intervention. I've seen many a dead body lying on a slab in the mortuary and it's never a pretty sight but the expression on Mallon's face is like no other I've seen before.

'My, my, not one of the best expressions I've seen in here (sniff, sniff),' says Andy.

All of us move closer to view what can only be described as the face of a man entering the abyss of the unknown. His eyes have a look of both terror and relief, relief at being saved 28 days before the Enchanter is due to collect, but terror at not knowing if he will be condemned to an eternity in the 'dark life', with his mouth wide open as if he's screaming with madness at the fate that beholds him. I see the four stab wounds on his body, which form the sign of the cross and have left him shrivelled and devoid of fluid. This is a man entering the void of eternal darkness with only the thinnest thread of hope to save him, namely Charity Holmes. Just as I was about to ask Andy for some time alone with the body, a voice, with a Southern American accent, echoes from behind. It's the coldest, darkest, most amoral voice I've ever heard.

'Who are you and what are you doing with my father's body?'

We turn around to see three people, two women and a man. The voice is that of the man in the middle.

'Mr Mallon's son, daughter and wife I presume?' I reply with a somewhat detached air about me for I know the evil that's standing in front of us.

5

Lost Soul

'You can presume as much as you like, I'm still waiting for an answer. Who are you and why are you here? What are you doing with my father's body?'

I instantly recognise him. He's the silhouette in Ma's vision who walks with the other woman and the 'Dark One' in the middle. The aura around him is that of a man with a cold hard heart, ruthless and amoral with the blackest of souls. He's about 6ft tall, aged about 25, extremely good-looking with thick short black hair, a powerful upright-looking physique, strong square chin with that all-American chiselled face. He stares straight at me with piercing dark eyes, which emanate the ugliness of his true nature, for behind those handsome features is evil incarnate. Immediately I sense that he's the owner of the cufflink.

'I'm Charity Holmes and I'm here at your father's request,' I reply. My psychic powers tell me that he already knows who I am because he's the one who has the protection of the Devil.

'So you're Charity Holmes, the famous psychic investigator. Well you're a little late, Charity, for father is beyond help now and my sister and mother would appreciate you leaving us to bury him in peace,' he replies without a trace of grief in his voice.

'How do you know my name? I'm sure we've never met and your father didn't mention you in his "visits" to me,' I ask, intrigued at how he will answer, because it's clear that he knows his father never 'visited' me while still mortal. There then follows one of those silent moments, as both he and his sister, a slim woman aged about 22, stare demonically through me. Their silence says everything. I know then that these two are the disciples of the 'Dark One' and I must be very careful if I'm to win this battle against evil.

'Enough of these questions. Alex and Lucy are not accountable to the likes of you and I won't tolerate you desecrating my husband's memory by performing your rituals in this way. It's not enough that he was brutally murdered. We now have to contend with charlatans like you trying to make money out of our grief,' the third woman says abruptly, speaking in a very strong American Southern belle accent. She is a highly attractive woman of about 55, with shoulder-length auburn hair, dark brown eyes, thin lips and a flawless line-free face, which has the look of the surgeon's scalpel. She is a woman, I sense, without any redeeming qualities, who takes rather than gives and loves only herself and power. Indeed the ideal woman to beget the disciples of the Devil. I step back for a second and take a long lingering look at the three of them and understand the tears of blood that poured from Mallon's eyes during his materialisation. The words 'my family despise me' never rang as true as they do at this moment. I know instantly that there is no love in the hearts of his children or wife, only avarice and loathing. Any one of these three would be pleased to see him dead. The mother is a woman who I suspect once loved with a passion and now hates with that very same passion. Not a woman you'd want to make an enemy of but a woman who's taught her children all the evils and none

56

of the virtues. I sense that the souls of these three are destined for the 'dark life'. But they are too greedy and arrogant to realise that the price they'll have to pay will be an eternity in Hell. The riches and power that they are currently enjoying in the mortal world will be but an atom of time in comparison.

'I understand your grief,' I say, knowing this really means nothing to them. 'Your father is a client of mine and the fact that he's no longer in the mortal world is of no relevance to me. I'm here to find information that will lead to his killer and also to the truth and I'll not stop until my client's wishes have been adhered to. If you're seeking the truth as well then none of us will have anything to fear.'

Robyn, Lizzy and Andy stand motionless, aware of the sense of menace and evil that emanates from these three, but most particularly from Alex and Lucy Mallon. Lucy Mallon moves slowly towards us, pushing past until she is standing over the body of her father. She looks down at him icily, running her hand down the side of his face, completely unmoved by his expression and says, 'Father, so this is your "avenging Angel" and her pathetic team. They'll not defeat the "True One" and what's his shall be collected.'

With those words all three of them stare directly into our eyes and we can feel their evil thoughts burning into our minds, trying to draw us towards them. I turn to see Andy slipping into a dark empty trance and quickly grab his arm to pull him back, knowing that the words that came from her mouth were really those of the Devil. I turn back quickly and walk straight towards Alex Mallon, standing so close to him that our eyes 'connect', and say without flinching, 'You're right, there's only one "True One" and he's on our side, and truth will always win, for hate destroys and love grows. You can't defeat that which always grows for it has no beginning and no end, so its strength never diminishes.'

For a few moments time seems to be endless, but suddenly I hear the dulcet tones of our old friend Chief Inspector Cranky spinning through the air.

'Since when have you been assigned to my investigative team, Miss Holmes?' he yells as he charges into the room with his face and moustache animated with sheer anger as his trusted sidekick Sergeant Dredge almost trips over himself trying to keep up with the raging bull in front of him. 'I've just come from the hotel where the so-called constable guarding the crime scene tells me that you're – quote – "an integral part of the investigative team and I'd be most upset if you weren't given full assistance in your investigation" – unquote. Now here you are again meddling into official police matters. I've a good mind to charge you and your so-called team with impersonating members of Her Majesty's Police Force and throw you all in the cells.'

'Excellent idea, Mr...?' are the eager words from Mrs Mallon, who's keen to see the back of us.

'Chief Inspector Cranky,' he replies, somewhat bemused by the woman standing before him. 'And you are?'

'Mrs Nancy Mallon, the deceased's wife, Chief Inspector, and these are my children Alex and Lucy, who I think you've already met when you interviewed them this morning. We've just arrived to find these "people" desecrating my husband's body with their psychic rituals and we'd be grateful if you could have them removed immediately,' she says in her superior Southern belle accent, while the other two so-called grief stricken children hold hands and smile demonically.

'No need to worry. We were just about to leave when you arrived, Chief Inspector,' I say, while turning to thank the now completely confused, shaking and continuously sniffing Andy, who I suspect is no more a psychic than the Chief Inspector.

'Just a minute, I haven't finished with you yet,' yells the Chief Inspector as the three of us quickly make our way past the Mallon clan, making sure to give them the famous Charity Holmes glance of contempt, which I reserve for the Devil's disciples. Robyn makes sure to smile sweetly at Sergeant Dredge, for she still has her mind set on picking his brains later.

'Can't stop, Chief Inspector, lots to do but no doubt we'll catch up later,' I shout back as the three of us race out of the building and quickly make our way back to the car with Robyn driving off quicker than a Formula One racing driver.

'Lord, oh Lord, if that family isn't the coldest and meanest lot I've ever met. Did you see their eyes? I felt as if they were boring right through my brain. Just as well I'd my rosary beads with me and "Himself" protecting us otherwise who knows what might have happened. Oh and that poor man's expression. What kind of horrors must have been going through his mind when he was dying. Wherever he's headed for in the spirit world he must have done something terrible to fear it so much,' says Lizzy, sounding all brave and full of bravado but underneath shaken and scared.

Then Robyn chips in, 'What a day: first we meet the "demon from Hell" and now we meet his disciples. I know I said I was prepared for anything but the deeper we dig into the life of Mallon the darker and more sinister it becomes. What kind of family are they? Those children – I get the shivers just thinking about them, and as for the so-called grief stricken wife Nancy, with the facelift from hell, I'd want to top myself if I was married to her.

59

One thing's for sure, those two delightful children are definitely the faded footprints in the bedroom and that Alex is most certainly the owner of the cufflink. The psychic aura I was getting from him was one of pure evil. There isn't one iota of human compassion or warmth in his soul, and his sister is a chip off the old block. Any one of those three could have murdered him without hesitating. In fact I wouldn't be surprised if they weren't all in it together. What do you think, Charity?'

'When Ma told me that evil was all around me and waiting I now know what she meant. Alex and Lucy Mallon are definitely the two mortals in my vision. I didn't see his wife there but somehow she's linked to his death as well. I'm convinced that they're not the killers but have a vested interest in his soul being collected by the Enchanter. If Mallon hadn't been murdered this morning they would have arranged his death twenty-eight days from now. Whoever killed him pre-empted their plans and now they have to make sure that his soul is not redeemed before the contract date. That makes them very dangerous and we must be extra vigilant if we're to succeed.'

We arrive back at the house and soon Aunt Lizzy is putting the kettle on while Robyn and I make our way into the lounge. I place a few logs on the fire and relight it so that we once again feel safe and warm while we digest the day's events. Aunt Lizzy comes back with a tray full of sandwiches and a large pot of tea and starts dishing them up while we continue to unravel the life of Stephen Mallon, our American spirit.

'What would Alex and Lucy Mallon gain from their father's death? Is it purely money or more than that? Because if it's just money then it wouldn't matter when he died as they would inherit presumably. So it has to be more than just money and the same must apply to Nancy his wife?' Robyn ponders.

'Exactly, spot on, Robyn. They must have a contract of their own and it's not with any mortal soul either,' I reply excitedly. 'They're expecting much greater riches than just money inherited from Mallon's estate. There's something about Alex and Lucy that's not right. They're not just disciples – they seem much more than that. They're too confident of their own success, almost as if their lives have been destined before they were born. The wife Nancy has no morals and therefore can easily be seduced by the "Dark One" for her soul is already full of darkness.'

Aunt Lizzy sits back in the large, soft chair beside the open fire scoffing away feeling much more content now she's back in her safe haven and says, 'If they didn't murder the American spirit ... then who did?'

'That's the sixty-four-dollar question, as they say, Lizzy,' I reply, snuggling up into the couch alongside Robyn and pouring myself another cup of tea.

'Well we know it's a woman, petite in size and that she had access to Mallon's room without having to break in,' states Robyn, who by now is over the shock of the day's events and thoroughly enjoying pitting our brains against the despicable trio.

'But that's all we know. Except I'm positive that she's not like the others and her motive for killing Mallon was love and not for greater riches,' I reply.

'How can murder be considered right? You're taking a life. What earthly reason could there be to condone the wickedest of acts?' pipes in Aunt Lizzy, puzzled by my obvious warmth towards this so-called murderer.

'You're right, Lizzy, murder is the most heinous of crimes but somehow in the case of our American spirit

I feel it was done not only to save his soul, but also to seek forgiveness and redemption for all his past sins. It was a pure act of love because to kill someone you love to save them must be the ultimate sacrifice,' I say, trying to justify my own feelings of protection that seem to be growing for the murderer.

Robyn sinks back further into the couch, contemplating everything that we've discussed and then remarks, 'Whoever this woman is she must be in both terrible mortal and spiritual danger. For no doubt the "Dark Trio", Alex, Lucy and Nancy, will want to see her dead for ruining their plans for the first of June. Plus murder, as you say, is such a heinous crime that her soul will be damned for ever. Whichever way you cut it she's lost. What a terrible price to pay for love.'

We sit for a few moments pondering Robyn's words, knowing that this woman is probably the only good thing to come into Mallon's life, yet just by loving him it will ultimately destroy her.

'Whoever she is and wherever she is we must find her before the Dark Trio otherwise both she and Mallon will be lost forever to the darkness,' I say thoughtfully while the three of us finish our tea and ponder our next move.

6

Love

I look at my watch and note that the time is almost 9.00 p.m. and mentally make a list of the next steps in the TIE. Just at that moment the telephone rings.

'I'll get it,' says Robyn, quickly leaping off the couch and grabbing the telephone. 'This is the residence of Charity Holmes, psychic investigator, her secretary Robyn Marlow speaking. How can I help?'

'Hi, Robyn, it's Sam, how are things at your end? I've certainly found some interesting stuff about your Mr Mallon out here. Is Charity there?'

'It's great to hear from you, Sam, and lots to report at this end, which I'm sure Charity will fill you in on in a minute. Just before I pass you over, when do think you'll be coming back?'

'I'm going to be out here for a least another week, which is why I'm ringing. There's something very strange about your Mr Mallon and I think it may be necessary for the RING to come out here.'

'I can't wait any longer, Robyn, put the phone on speaker so we can all hear,' I say, eager to learn what Sam has found out. 'It's really good to hear your voice, old girl, missing you like mad. When are you coming back and what have you found out?'

'Not so much of the old, thank you, and missing you

too. Well I've got lots to tell you so you'd better park yourself comfortably. But first, before I begin, what about your end? What's happening there?'

'Well, we've visited the crime scene and the mortuary to view the body. Met the so-called grieving family, alias wife Nancy, son Alex and daughter Lucy who Robyn has nicknamed the "Dark Trio". They're definitely in the frame somewhere but I don't think they killed him. There's another female in the picture who I suspect is the murderer but somehow feel strangely warm towards her. I'm waiting for Monty to ring to see what he and Jack have found out. Oh, and I've had visitations from the spirit world, which I'll tell you about when I see you but suffice it to say we're on a timescale of less than twenty-eight days. We need to solve this mystery before ten-thirty in the morning on the first of June otherwise all will be lost.'

'No need to panic. After all, the world was created in less time,' Sam replies in her usual quick-witted patter that flows easily between the two of us. The three of us then settle back, eager to hear what Sam has to report.

'Firstly, this Stephen Mallon was very well known and connected out here, especially in the South. He dealt in the money market by buying and selling stocks and shares in all sorts of businesses. He also had a reputation for acquiring companies by let's say unpopular methods and then selling them on at a profit. His business offices are all over America, one here in New York, and others in South Carolina, San Francisco, Texas and Washington DC. He was also a congressman, and according to my sources here, which I am not at liberty to disclose as the Mallon family are feared out here and people don't openly speak against them, used that position mercilessly to gain power over people. His wife Nancy and two children, Alex and Lucy, are extremely cold, ruthless people who

64

will use any method to achieve their goals. Most fear Alex Mallon more than his father. In fact I can't find one single person out here who has a good word to say about him or the Mallon family. There's a business partner Donald Coleman who owns thirty-five per cent of the company, which is called Mallon Enterprises.

'Apparently he was engaged to Nancy twenty-five years ago until Mallon came along and stole her from him when she fell pregnant with Alex. According to my sources he's a bitter, weak and shallow man who drinks and gambles. Nancy's father offered him the partnership in the business fifteen years ago just before he died to stop Stephen Mallon gaining complete control of the company. It would appear that originally Mallon Enterprises was called Cane Enterprises as the company belonged to Nancy's father Douglas Cane, who disliked Stephen Mallon intensely. He never wanted her to marry him, so, just before he died, and his only child, Nancy, inherited the company, he gave thirty-five per cent of the company to Donald Coleman. Donald Coleman hated Stephen Mallon with a passion for taking Nancy from him. He's never married and was constantly looking for ways to destroy him.

'Apparently when Stephen Mallon turned up twenty-five years ago, Cane Enterprises was struggling. He subsequently seduced Nancy and persuaded her to convince her father to let him buy in to the company in order to save it. She was passionately in love with him so convinced her father to let him become a partner in the company by buying forty per cent of the shares. Once in, things rapidly changed and Douglas Cane soon realised he'd made a terrible mistake, but it was too late – Stephen Mallon was taking over the company and running it his way. So the only way Douglas Cane could keep Mallon from swallowing up the entire company was to leave the thirty-five per cent to Donald Coleman in his will, the other twenty-five per cent being left to Nancy. To make sure that Mallon never got his hands on the shares, it was stipulated that if Donald Coleman died or left the company in any way then his shares would automatically go into a charitable trust. This trust was to be set up separately under the name of "The Douglas Charitable Trust" and would run for one hundred and fifty years. All dividends and monies received from the shares in this trust would be used to help the poor and needy. It had strict terms and conditions setting out the aims and objectives of the trust: how the money was to be spent and who the trustees were to be running it. All trustees had to be volunteers and not connected or related to Mallon in any way. Therefore Mallon was stuck with Donald Coleman as a partner, and although the men hated each other, they were effectively bound together by greed and hate.'

'The deeper we dig into our American spirit's past the more corrupt and sinister his life and family seem to be. It appears that almost anyone he came into contact with or touched in his life, including his own family, would want him dead. There doesn't seem to be any redeeming quality about him and yet from my visions I know I have been chosen to seek not only justice for his murder but redemption for his soul. What is it about this man that makes me feel compassion when I hear and see such terrible things about him?' I say, interrupting Sam, for my heart is sinking from the sheer burden of trying to find at least one redeeming quality about Mallon.

'Well, there is more to come,' Sam replies, catching her breath before continuing.

'I've checked right back into his past but everything stops when he's twenty years old. Before that date there's no record of him anywhere. It seems as if he became

Stephen Mallon forty years ago and the first twenty years of his life didn't exist. I'm at a blank as what to do next and strongly feel that your presence is needed out here if we're to find out any more.'

'That's intriguing, Sam, for in his materialisation Mallon said that he was visited by a spirit called the Enchanter in a series of dreams when he was twenty years old. In these dreams the Enchanter offered him all that he desired and more. But in order to achieve this he had to sell his soul in a contract to the Enchanter, who I believe is the Devil himself. The collection date of this contract is the first of June. Therefore we need to discover who he was before that date and whose soul he stole to become Stephen Mallon.'

At that point Robyn chips in, hoping that this trip to America is now on the cards. 'What about the other woman? Have you discovered a link between a third woman, perhaps a lover out there, Sam?'

Sam pauses for a few moments then replies, 'Yes, there's something else. There's rumours that he had a secret love-child who would be about twenty years old now, but no one can actually say who or where she is. It's reported that Nancy has been employing detectives for years trying to find both this other child and information about his past. It didn't take long for her passionate love for him to turn to hate. Their marriage, it appears, was purely based on money and power. He gained power through obtaining her company and connections, and she keeps her wealth and status in society by staying married to him. Again, a partnership not joined in love but avarice. My sources inform me that Nancy and her children are constantly trying to find ways, like Donald Coleman, to get control of Mallon Enterprises by eliminating their father.'

There's a moment of silence while we all try to digest

67

Sam's information. 'At last we have a connection to the third woman, thin as it may be, whose footprints were etched in Mallon's blood in his hotel bedroom. You're right, Sam, it definitely calls for a visit. We need to find out who this woman is and get to her before the "Dark Trio" otherwise I fear she'll be joining her father fairly quickly. Also I sense that there's another family somewhere in the past connected to Mallon, which has something to do with another vision I had about a young boy playing by a stream.'

'What boy? What stream?' Sam interrupts, excitedly, for the more she hears, the more her adrenalin starts pumping at the thought of the RING working together again on a case.

'Ma showed me a vision of a tall, gangly boy aged about fifteen playing by a stream who suddenly disappears into darkness. Somehow I know he's connected to Mallon's past and we need to discover who he is, for this boy is the beginning of Stephen Mallon's journey – of that I'm sure,' I say, knowing that this will require all our resources if we are to find what no one else has managed to in the last 40 years: the secret of Stephen Mallon's past.

'I suspect your American spirit's past is going to turn out to be one BIG DARK SECRET, which will cause no end of turbulence once it's let out,' says Sam, as she prepares to join forces with the RING to uncover his past.

'I need to speak to Monty first to see what he and Jack have turned up and whether they're able to join Robyn and me in America,' I say, looking at Robyn who by now is highly animated like a school girl on her first trip abroad, which I fear can't be said of Aunt Lizzy who I sense feels a bit left out as she isn't included in my journey to America.

'Great, I will wait to hear from you soon, and don't

worry, I'm staying at the house of an old friend out here so accommodation is not a problem. Love yah all and see you soon.'

With that Sam is gone and once again the three of us are left pondering even more riddles in the life of our American spirit.

I turn quickly to Aunt Lizzy, saying, 'I know you are disappointed at not being included in the trip to America but I need you here, Lizzy. I need to know what's going on while we're away. Don't forget the "Dark Trio" is still here and for all we know the other woman as well, so it's very important that you keep your nose to the ground to form the link back here while we're in America.'

'That's right, Lizzy, we won't be here so it's all down to you while we're away,' pipes in Robyn, quickly, knowing how disappointed she'd have felt if I hadn't included her in the American investigation.

'No problem, girls, you know you can rely on me. I'll keep a sharp eye on things. I've formed a good contact with one of the receptionists at the hotel so can do a bit more digging about to see what the "Dark Trio's" up to while yah are away,' replies Aunt Lizzy, who by now feels very important, as it seems she'll be handling everything single-handedly from her end.

Feeling better about Aunt Lizzy, I then proceed to follow the next step of the TIE.

'OK, Robyn, I need you to check the airlines for departure times for New York for the day after tomorrow, preferably early morning as we don't have much time to spare. I will talk to Monty tonight to see what Special Operations and Jack's contact in forensics at Scotland Yard have found out. Hopefully all being well he and Jack will be arriving tomorrow. If he's finished his debriefing on the Poleaxe case then you can finalise plane tickets for the four of us. Also see if you can arrange to meet Sergeant Dredge and prise some more information about the case from him, for I'm sure Chief Inspector Cranky is holding something back. As it's getting late, I suggest you get some sleep for you'll need to be up with the birds if we're to complete our quest before the first of June.'

Robyn leaps off the couch, eager to retire to her bed and sleep so tomorrow arrives quicker, and the next stage of the TIE can begin. 'Don't worry, I'll be on it first thing in the morning and will have Sergeant Dredge drooling and spilling the beans before we get on that plane.'

With that both Robyn and Aunt Lizzy make their way to their respective beds; Robyn to her tiny little basement apartment, which she has lovingly made her home since coming to stay with me last year, and Aunt Lizzy to her large bedroom on the second floor. With the both of them now safely tucked up for the night I make my way back to my quiet room to await Monty's call and write my notes up on the case so far. Being an insomniac I only need a few hours sleep each night (psychic dreams excluded), so always end each day by writing up the events that have unfolded in my diary. I've done this since childhood, which has become an essential and comforting part of my life. Time seems to drift by quite effortlessly when I'm at my desk writing up my notes. When I'm finished I sit back to consider what we know and what still needs to be discovered.

First: What we know.

Suspects: We have the 'Dark Trio', Nancy, Alex and Lucy. We have Mallon's business partner, Donald Coleman, and the boy in my vision. Then there's the prime suspect, the secret daughter. All of these had reason and motive so see Mallon dead. But only two I would suspect would have reason to see him dead before 1st June, namely the secret daughter and possibly the boy by the stream if he's still alive. The others, I would bet my reputation on it, would only benefit if his soul is claimed by the Enchanter at 10.30 a.m. on 1st June.

Second: What needs to be discovered.

Who was Mallon before the age of 20? Whose soul did he steal to become Stephen Mallon? Who is the boy by the stream? What connection has he to Mallon? Does he have another family that existed before he was 'reborn' at the age of 20? If they discovered his new life would they benefit from his death? Who is the secret daughter? Where and who is her mother? Is she a suspect in his murder? Why do his children Alex and Lucy have the protection of the Devil? What do they have to gain when Mallon's soul is collected by the Enchanter? What contract have they entered into with the Devil to have his protection? Why is Alex Mallon, according to Sam, more feared than his father? What does Nancy have to gain from her husband's death on 1st June that she doesn't have already? Does she have a contract with the Enchanter? What would Donald Coleman gain from his death? Surely not Nancy, for I doubt if he would be good enough for her now. Lastly, why has Mallon been given a second chance? What is it about him that makes his soul worth saving? There are still so many unanswered questions. I keep trying to focus on what Ma told me in her materialisation: 'Follow the vision and you'll know the truth. Remember, even the good fall from grace. God always protects the good and fights evil. Search for the good to destroy evil.'

'Search for the good to destroy evil.' I keep repeating

71

those words over and over again in my mind. 'Search for the good. I'm convinced this is his secret love-child, who, although I fear is his killer, somehow I know is the good in my search. Also the young gangly boy by the stream with the pale complexion and deep black eyes who is simple and trusting with a true heart. He's also the good I sense in my search, and when I find him I'll know the answer, which will enable me to destroy the evil.'

Evil: The Dark Trio, Alex, Lucy and Nancy, are definitely in that category. Alex and Lucy are the silhouettes in my vision who walk hand in hand with the Enchanter (Devil) in the centre, who's already shown his hand in his materialisation at the hotel when Robyn and I used the cufflink. Nancy has made some sort of deal with the Devil yet she hasn't appeared in any of my visions, which leads me to believe her soul is still 'untouched' and therefore redeemable. Donald Coleman could be in collusion with the 'Dark Trio', but somehow I don't see him as truly evil, but will reserve judgement on him until we meet. I now see my quest clearly: find and save the good, namely the secret love-child and the boy in my vision by the stream, and destroy the evil – the Enchanter and his disciples.

7

The Enchanter

I glance at my watch – it's nearly 1.00 a.m. and once again time seems to float by when I'm in deep thought. Just at that moment the telephone rings and, sure enough, I hear the soft, soothing voice of my beloved Monty.

'How's my beautiful psychic spud then?' Secretly I love his little nickname, for whenever I hear it I feel all safe and warm inside.

'All spud out and ready for bed. Have you finished your debriefing? It seems an eternity since you left, my love.'

'All done and dusted, and I can't wait to see your gorgeous smile and look into those beautiful blue eyes. Jack and I will be catching the early train tomorrow and should be home before midday so tell Lizzy there'll be two hungry hunks to feed.'

Whenever I hear Monty's voice I just can't imagine how I managed to exist before he came in to my life. He's my soul mate and part of me and without him I just don't feel complete. We are as one and even though our careers mean we sometimes spend time apart, just knowing he's in my life makes everything right. Tonight I'll sleep more easily knowing that tomorrow he'll be holding me close. For no matter how great or powerful my gift, it's nothing compared to the strength I feel with

Monty's love. To be loved and to love with such completeness is the greatest gift of all.

'Lizzy will be happy. She loves cooking for you two. Did you manage to find anything out about Mallon and how about Jack's friend in forensics at Scotland Yard? Any juicy bits there?' I ask eagerly, for Monty and Jack never let me down and always come up with some interesting bits of information whenever I'm investigating a case.

'That's my girl, no matter how tired you are or late it is your little brain is always ticking away looking for and trying to solve the next clue.'

'Oh, stop teasing me, Monty, you know I can't wait until you arrive tomorrow, or should I say later on today. I'll go potty if you don't tell me what you've found out.'

I can hear Monty giggling away at the other end with Jack sniggering in the background. The two of them are like big kids who love teasing me when they think they know something I don't. It's that male superiority thing they always go through whenever I'm eager for information on a case.

'Well, spud, your Mr Mallon was certainly a dark one. I had my contacts at the Secret Service do a thorough check on him, his family and his business dealings. He is or should I say was a very shady character indeed. Once I started digging around I found out that his family and company have been under surveillance by both the American and British Governments. It looks like they're involved in the trafficking of guns and military weapons, buying and selling to the highest bidders. His son Alex seems to be the main player in this. His daughter Lucy also seems to have a sideline of her own, smuggling drugs using Mallon Enterprises as a front. This investigation has been going on for the last three years but whenever either side gets close to nabbing them they always come unstuck. Somehow the Mallon family always seem to be one step ahead. They appear to have contacts everywhere and corruption at the highest level. But neither the American nor British Special Investigative Teams on the case can find who or where these leaks are.'

'My God, this man and his family just seem to get worse and worse. Just one peace of good news about him would be welcome at the moment,' I say, interrupting Monty, for I'm desperately trying to cling on to the hope that I will discover something redeemable about Mallon soon.

'Ah, but the best bit is yet to come, spud,' says Monty. 'There doesn't seem to be any record of him prior to the age of twenty. We can trace him back through a series of companies that he either owned or was involved in to a small town called Homerville in South Carolina. It seems that he suddenly appeared as an enforcer for a local loan shark forty years ago when he was twenty. Before long he was running the company and then the so-called owner had an accident, whereby he was burnt alive in one of his own warehouses. They never solved the case, though the police records indicate that Mallon was their prime suspect. Shortly afterwards he took over the loan company and within a couple of years he was running the town and the people in it. He seemed to acquire power, riches and respectability fairly rapidly after that. The strange thing is that when I telephoned the local sheriff in Homerville to discuss Mallon he clammed up and refused to talk about him. I get the feeling that something very strange happened in that town and I for one would like to know what?'

I listen intently to Monty, for now we are getting a little closer to the past of Mallon. Now we have the name of a town, Homerville, where his new life seemed to begin when he was 20. 'I had a call from Sam tonight who's in America and she drew the same blank as you, in that no one out there seems to know about Mallon prior to the age of twenty. But now we have a connection in Homerville. Sam wants us to join her out there and I think it would be a good idea. How do you feel about a trip to Homerville in the next couple of days? Sam will meet us in New York where she's staying at a friend's house. We can check out Mallon Enterprises in New York and then move on to Homerville,' I say, knowing that Monty is now well and truly hooked and will be eager to discover more about our mysterious American spirit.

'Jack and I are more than keen to find out more about your mysterious spirit and his family. Solving this one would be a feather in our cap, especially as neither government departments on either side of the Atlantic have managed to do it so far, so book us in, spud.'

'Great, I'll get Robyn to sort the arrangements out tomorrow.'

I can hear Jack in the background chivvying away at Monty, obviously eager to pass on his bit of knowledge. Then I hear his tough masculine voice on the line, which belies the tender heart that beats beneath. Everything about his manner is the opposite of Monty, tough and hard in appearance with that no-nonsense ex-army manner. A man who has seen and been through a lot in his forty-five years but somehow retains that honour-bound persona. A man I'd entrust my own soul to without hesitation. He's indeed the purest of friends.

'Good morning, Miss Charity.' He always calls me that with his old-fashioned manners. 'And I hope you are fit and fine.'

'I am indeed, Jack, and as usual you sound as resilient as ever. So what juicy bit of info have you discovered about our mysterious American spirit?'

'We've a very strange one here. I met with my contact

76

at Scotland Yard who works in forensics and was involved in the post-mortem. This case has become very hush-hush and the report has been marked "eyes closed, top level only". The only reason I've managed to find out any information is because this chap owes me a big favour and I've called it in.'

Immediately my brain goes into overdrive like a sponge waiting to absorb every little piece of knowledge that Jack is about to enlighten me with. 'What do you mean by "eyes closed, top level only"?' I ask, intrigued.

'It means that only the very highest level of the investigation team will be allowed to see the full report. The investigating officers on the case will see a dummy report, which will exclude what I'm about to tell you. It would seem that the powers above don't know how to handle what's been discovered during the post-mortem and so have chosen to keep it secret. Not even the Chief Inspector running the investigation knows what I'm about to tell you.'

Ah, so I know something that Chief Inspector Cranky doesn't. Oh how delicious those words sound. For I'm sure I can use that to my advantage later on when no doubt our paths will cross again. I find it's always useful to have another card up my sleeve when dealing with men like Cranky. 'What is it that's so extraordinary that even the Chief Inspector hasn't been told?' I ask eagerly.

'Well, it appears that even though this Mr Mallon was about sixty years old and both his face and outer body were ageing, his internal organs weren't. Firstly, his blood doesn't match any known human type. They can't trace it anywhere. It's not of the animal variety or any other species known to man. Also his body was almost completely drained of blood. Secondly, all his internal organs are in peak condition. They appear to belong to a man forty years younger. My contact said they have never seen anything like it before. It seems that outside, his skin and tissue were ageing, although he looked extremely well preserved for a man of his years, but internally he's not aged at all. Thirdly, when checking for his medical records he doesn't appear to have any. There's no record of him ever seeing a doctor or medical practitioner of any kind, and there's no record of him ever attending a hospital or needing any kind of medical attention. They've drawn a complete blank. Also they can't trace a birth certificate or place of birth. It's as if he just arrived. He seems to have come from nothing and nowhere. Lastly, although he has been dead since four yesterday morning, his body is still warm as if in some way he's still alive. Yet he's not breathing or functioning in any way.

'My contact stated that it seemed as if he was in hibernation, waiting to wake up from a deep sleep. There you have it, Miss Charity, one very strange corpse indeed.'

'Once again, Jack, you've excelled yourself. Everything you've told me confirms what I've already heard from Sam and seen in my visions. Our Mr Mallon was "reborn" forty years ago when he entered into a contract with a spirit called the Enchanter. It's imperative that we visit Homerville, where it all began, if we are to uncover his dark secret.'

'I'm with you on that one, Miss Charity, and will be driving Monty up in the morning. Until tomorrow, then, sleep well and be safe.'

'The same to you, Jack, and if you could just pass the old man over to me before you go.'

'Hey, who's calling who old? I'm in my prime thank you very much. I love you to bits and catch you tomorrow.'

'Love you too, darling.'

With that Monty and Jack are gone. I quickly complete

my notes adding the latest revelations about Mallon to my list of endless questions. With that done I make my way to bed feeling very weary, and, unusually for me, tired enough to sleep through the night, or should I say morning, noting that it's already gone two. Somehow I don't think I'll be suffering from my usual insomnia tonight, and gently drift into a cosy, warm sleep, comforted by the thought that I'll be seeing Monty tomorrow.

'Up yah get, darling, the sun's out and the birds are singing,' bellows Aunt Lizzy, ripping the bed covers off. Boy I'm glad that Monty's back today, as she wouldn't dare pull the covers off when he's in bed. Here we are again, I think to myself, getting ready for another day and another battle between the dark and light that exists in both the mortal and spirit world. Sometimes I wonder what my life would have been like if I didn't have my gift. But whatever the battles and dark forces I may come up against in my career as an inceptor, I wouldn't have it any other way. What a privileged life I've led, and what wonders I've seen and experienced. I need the excitement of new challenges and battles each day. It's my destiny and how I love every minute of it.

'Good morning everyone,' I say, entering the kitchen as Robyn and Lizzy tuck into a big fry up.

'Ditto,' Robyn replies. 'Well, I've managed to sort everything. First, I've rescheduled all your appointments so that we're free for the next month. Second, I booked the four of us on a flight for New York early tomorrow morning. Third, I've arranged to meet Sergeant Dredge for lunch today to see what I can extract from him. Lastly I've telephoned Sam who will be picking us up at the airport.'

'How on earth did I manage to plan my days before

you came into my life. You're a wonder, but then it's in the genes, isn't it, Lizzy?'

'You're not wrong there, girl. When are the lads back and will I be cooking dinner for five tonight?'

'Absolutely, two very hungry hunks was their description.'

'Well, I'd better be doing some extra shopping today in between my sleuthing; housekeeper one minute and detective the next – I amaze myself sometimes,' says Aunt Lizzy in her chirpy 'I'm full of myself' Irish brogue, as she quickly tidies away the breakfast dishes before getting ready to go out.

Just at that moment two hunky male figures stand astride the kitchen door looking their usual insouciant selves and immediately my heart skips a beat when I hear that deep, gentle voice.

'Put the kettle on, Lizzy, before we die of thirst and some of your delicious toast wouldn't go amiss either, old girl.'

Then I feel Monty's strong arms around me and his gentle kiss on my lips, and once again I feel complete. Jack and Monty make themselves comfortable while Aunt Lizzy fusses around like a mother hen for she loves them both like they were her own flesh and blood.

How good it feels to have all of us together, the RING almost complete. As we sit at the table laughing and chatting away I can feel their love and strength. Sometimes, just like now, if I look carefully I can see the most beautiful aura emanating from and around us. It's like a soft rainbow of colours encompassing us all in its protection and warmth. If only everyone could see what I see when they're surrounded by their friends and loved ones. This must be what the afterlife (Heaven) must feel like and why those spirits who are not able to reach it feel such despair. How absolutely wretched our American spirit must feel to be so close and yet so far from his rainbow of eternal happiness. I cling on to that thought while we sit and chat, knowing that we're his only salvation in his battle for redemption. Time drifts by effortlessly and before long Monty and Jack are brought up to speed on everything: from Robyn's first encounter by telephone with Mallon to his subsequent materialisation and the Chief Inspector's visit; from Ma's visions of divine intervention and our visit to the crime scene at the hotel to our visit to the mortuary to see Mallon's body and meeting the 'Dark Trio'. And finally Sam's report from America.

'Well, spud, one thing's for sure, whatever clients we get at Special Operations, they never even come close to matching yours. You certainly can pick them. We may be a bit out of our depth with this one, though, for I'm not sure what or whom we are dealing with here. If we're battling against the personification of Evil I'm afraid we may not be up to it this time. Are you sure you want to continue? Is the RING strong enough? The battle against the dark forces out there can't always be won and we must be aware of that before we enter into its jaws,' says Monty.

I look at Jack with that strong masculine frame of his and see the fear in his eyes, for although he's seen and experienced many terrible things during his time in the Army, fighting the darkest of evils in the spirit world wasn't one of them.

'You know I'm one hundred and fifty per cent behind you, Miss Charity, but I agree with Monty on this one. I'm not sure we can succeed. For one thing why are we bothering to save the soul of the likes of this Stephen Mallon? Everything I've heard about him so far leads me to believe retribution is due and he deserves his fate, also the Mallon family or so-called "Dark Trio" are not the kind that lose. They take whatever they want regardless of the consequences and from what I've heard here today have the protection of the Devil himself. What can the RING do against him? What ammunition have we got to fight him with? We are only six mortals. He has the power of infinite evil. What weapons can we use against that?'

I listen tenderly to what Jack has to say, noting that his usual strong voice now sounds more mellow and occasionally fearful. Everything that Jack and Monty have said is right. Any normal mortal wouldn't even consider entering into battle with the supremely dark satanic forces of Beelzebub, Lucifer, Satan or the Devil, whichever name we mortals choose to call him.

'I hear you both and sense the fear that you feel and more, for I know what dark forces we're up against and the consequences that'll be paid if we fail. But this battle is not of our choosing. It has chosen us. When the spirit calls upon you there is no choice. With the help of the RING I have to complete this quest. We can't walk away. The American spirit will not let us. God himself has spoken to me through his visions of divine intervention. I have no choice. I must continue until the end. I know that through mine and Robyn's psychic powers and the love and strength of the RING we'll succeed. We've been chosen for a reason. We have the ultimate weapon, the power of the Supreme Being, the creator and ruler of life itself. He will protect and guide us on our quest. I know we'll win this battle against the Lord of Darkness.'

There's the most chilling moment of silence that passes between us, one that I've never felt before. I sense their anguish and fear. Then Monty takes my hand and seals his ring against mine. He looks deep into my eyes and smiles. No words are spoken, for none are needed. I feel his love and strength and that says everything. With that we all sit together, join our rings and become as one.

Then Robyn leaps to her feet, saying, 'Well, I'd better double check the flights and arrival times for Kennedy Airport tomorrow and then I'll be off to see Sergeant Dredge. Catch you all later.' Then quicker than a flash of lightning, she's gone.

'I've got lots to do as well, so will be off now. Don't worry, my darlings, the powers that be have spoken. He's chosen you, Charity, my precious, and that's it. We're in His hands now,' says Aunt Lizzy as she gets ready to go shopping and sleuthing.

Jack senses that Monty and I need to be alone for a while so tactfully mumbles something about making final arrangements for tomorrow's trip as he leaves the two of us alone. No more words are needed as we fumble our way to the bedroom.

While Monty's in the bathroom getting ready for tonight I lay back on the bed smiling and quietly humming to myself, feeling all warm and secure. Suddenly I feel an icy-cold chill in the room, as the door to the bathroom slams shut. Monty always leaves it slightly ajar so we can chat while getting ready. I try to move to get to the door but my body isn't responding. I feel as if I'm in a dream where I can see and feel everything around me but my body's frozen in time. I hear Monty banging on the bathroom door trying to get out while shouting my name.

'Charity, are you OK? What's going on? I can't get the door open. Where are you?'

Then the bedroom door slams shut as I see Jack rushing towards it, but he's too late as he bangs and pulls on the door, desperately trying to get in as I hear his cries.

'Miss Charity, Monty, what's happening? Can you hear me? I can't open the door? Are you both OK? Answer me if you can?'

'I'm here but can't move. I feel a presence entering the room. Don't do anything. I'll be all right,' I say, trying to comfort both Monty and Jack.

'I feel helpless. I can't get the door open. I'm afraid for you, my darling,' shouts Monty. I sense the fear and panic in his voice. I feel his pain but can do nothing to help him, Jack or myself. Whatever is about to appear has separated the three of us to make our connection weaker. I must face this visitor alone. I'm rooted to the bed and look around the room, which seems to be closing in on me as the walls become dark with shadowy, ghoulish figures seeping in and out of them with their satanic cries piercing through my ears. The whole room takes on a Gothic, barbarous appearance as if I'm being transported into another world, a supernatural world, full of beings and forces unlike any I've ever seen or felt before. Then the walls start to come alive and hollow out into a long tunnel that whirls continuously into endless darkness as I see him walking towards me through the dark whirling tunnel.

A tall handsome figure emanating power and strength approaches and as he moves closer I can see the splendour of his coat astride his powerful frame. Its colours are magnificent in their multitude, shining like a golden rainbow, which is about to swallow you up in its glory. As he draws closer I can feel my whole body and soul being encompassed by his presence, willing me to join him in his world. Immediately I know this is the Enchanter. His voice is powerful and strong, yet soothing and alluring at the same time, as the words flow off his tongue like liquid gold, surrounding and enticing me with their promises of power and riches.

'The time has come, Charity. Why waste your powers on such ineffectual beings. Come and join me, and your powers will know no limits. Feel the power grow within you and succumb to its glory. Come with me, Charity, and know the wonders of the "dark life". Just hold out your hand and I will lead you to your destiny. Come, Charity. You know it's what you really desire. Let me give you your ultimate wish. Whatever you ask shall be yours. Just hold my hand, Charity, and feel the power of the Dark One. He desires you. He's waiting. Join him, Charity. Become one with Him.'

Part of me knows that what I see before me is just an illusion. For the Enchanter is but a vision of your own desires and dreams. He's not real. He's a manifestation of your own inner thoughts. He's the beast within us all. He enters your mind and corrupts your thoughts in order to steal your soul. He offers you everything but gives you nothing. Lose your soul to him and you're lost forever to the darkness. I know this and yet I find myself inexplicably drawn towards him with every part of me trying to resist.

I can hear Monty and Jack's voices in the distance as they desperately try to gain entry into the room, yet I'm unable to move. As he glides closer and closer towards me with his hand stretched out I feel myself slowly rising from the bed and floating with my hand held out ready to touch his. I'm frantic with fear for I know if our hands touch I have sealed the contract and will be lost forever. I call upon my gift to close my eyes and concentrate my mind. I mustn't give in. My gift must not desert me now. I'm stronger than him, for my mind and body is real. He's but an illusion. Believe in the real and discard the illusion and nothing can touch me. I repeat Monty's name over and over again in my mind. I call his name out loud. I visualize his body next to mine. I feel his arms around me giving me his love and strength. I think only of him. Slowly I close my mind and thoughts to the words of the Enchanter. His voice becomes colder and darker as his illusion slowly fades away and his power starts to weaken.

Then I open my eyes and see him for what he really is, as I continue to call Monty's name and feel his love. Suddenly both doors open with Monty and Jack rushing in with such a force only to be transfixed and almost spellbound by what they see. By now I'm floating in the middle of the room with my hands stretched out almost touching the Enchanter. His coat is no longer magnificent in its colours but ragged and crawling with serpents. Monty and Jack suddenly find their strength and move swiftly to pull me back into the middle of them, Monty protecting me with his love and Jack with a gun he's grabbed from his room, which bless his heart would be useless against the Devil. We look at the vision floating before us, no longer a handsome, beguiling man, but an ugly beast. The Horned Goat of Mendes with great bat wings. Half man half beast with dark satanic eyes, the Devil incarnate. Evil personified. Then he speaks and the room echoes with the black demonic hollowness of his voice.

'How touching. It seems your gift and so-called power of love has saved you this time, Charity. But you were nearly mine. You will succumb. All you mortals are weak. You will join me. You will be mine.'

Then he slowly disappears into the whirling tunnel of darkness from whence he came, leaving behind the coldest, emptiest, most chilling laugh I've ever heard.

'What the hell was that? What are we up against? I felt completely powerless. How are we going to fight that?' Monty says, gripping me so tightly that I can hardly breathe. I can feel his body trembling. I've never known him so afraid. Even Jack is visibly shaken, the hard no-nonsense ex-SAS officer desperately trying to appear in control while his whole body is quaking with a combination of fear and shock. I understand their fear, for I felt it racing through me as I floated helplessly towards my fate.

'But we did win,' I reply, feeling my strength returning. 'He may be all-powerful in the darkness of his world where only pain and suffering are known, but when he enters the mortal world he becomes weak. He enters a world where there's light, hope and love. All of which can destroy him. He only survives by feeding on our inner beast, the dark side of our nature. Give yourself over to your dark side and he wins. Hold onto the side of love and truth and he loses. Our love is stronger than his darkness.'

I stand there watching Monty and Jack give each other their special little smiles. The ones they do when they don't have an answer to a problem, but are not completely convinced that I do either. Then Jack asks, 'Why did he want you, Miss Charity? I thought he was after the soul of your American spirit?'

'He is, Jack, but he knows that we're a threat. With my powers and the strength of the RING we are a force to be reckoned with. His attempt to seduce me over to the dark side today proves that we're stronger than him. He will continue to come after us. We must solve this mystery before the first of June. Only then will we have the power to destroy him and his disciples.'

Monty and Jack smile nervously, indicating that maybe the RING has bitten off more than it can chew this time.

'Anything happen while I've been fending off the advances of the twitching Sergeant Dredge?' Robyn asks, as she charges into the room.

The three of us smile quietly to each other, signalling that maybe she needn't know the details of the last few minutes.

'Not much, kiddo, been rather dull here. Hope you've got something interesting to report,' Monty replies as we make our way back to the lounge to hear Robyn's news.

'I would like it known before I begin my report that I

endured two hours of eyeballing and twitching from the dreaded Sergeant Dredge in order to extract this information.'

'Duly noted. Your actions in the line of duty will unequivocally reserve you a place in the afterlife,' I reply, giggling while Monty and Jack help themselves to their favourite malt whisky, grinning away at Robyn hamming it up. Robyn then eagerly relays her report.

'Firstly, Jack, your contact in forensics at Scotland Yard was right; none of the investigating team, including Chief Inspector Cranky, knows the true report from the post-mortem. But there was one very strange thing that happened when Dredge and Cranky were at the crime scene. Now the only person to experience it is Sergeant Dredge and he hasn't told the Chief Inspector or anybody else. I only managed to extract this from him because he thinks it will curry favour with me and also because of my psychic connections. While checking out the crime scene, Sergeant Dredge or Glen, as we're on first name basis now, saw something strange happen to the body. He was standing over it, looking for clues, when suddenly it began to metamorphose into another person. His face began to change from a sixty-year-old man to a young teenage boy. According to Glen his whole body started to glow and rise slightly from the bed. Then the boy's eyes opened and looked directly at him. He said he'd never forget the way they seemed to bore into his mind. They were jet-black and willing him to look deeper into them. As he looked he could see shadowy figures. There was a young boy playing by a waterfall. He looked exactly like the boy now lying dead on the bed. Then floating above him was another figure. Unlike the boy this figure was glowing with a white translucent light all around it. It appeared to be a knight in full armour with huge wings and wielding an unsheathed sword in his right hand. He seemed to signify all that was righteous and good, emanating justice and power. The boy looked up at this magnificent glowing knight and reached out to touch it just as the vision disappeared.

'Next Glen felt a hand grabbing his wrist tightly, pulling him down onto the bed until both faces were almost touching. In a whisper he heard the words "save me". He pulled himself away, wrenching the hand from his wrist. Within seconds the body changed back to that of Stephen Mallon. He looked around the room and saw that no one else had seen this metamorphosis. Understandably he didn't tell anybody about his experience, especially Cranky, for fear of being laughed at. But talking to him, it was clear that it was very real to him and so consequently he now has a rather different perspective on the case than his Chief Inspector. He's willing to be more open minded with regard to our involvement and will keep me informed of any new developments if I'll do the same. I think he feels that we can help him solve the case more quickly than the Chief Inspector, who it appears has drawn a blank so far. Also it wouldn't do his promotion prospects any harm. I don't need to use any of my intuitive senses to see that he would love to be released from the Chief Inspector's clutches.'

Robyn then settles back into the chair, smiling smugly, while congratulating herself on a job well done. Jack hands her a well-earned gin and tonic (her favourite tipple) while we sit digesting everything.

'What do you make of that then, spud?' quips Monty, grinning away, while pouring Jack and himself their third malt whisky.

'The vision of the boy by the waterfall that Sergeant Dredge describes is the same as mine. Now that he's materialised into the body of our American spirit it confirms my original belief that the two are connected.

The knight in armour with wings wielding an unsheathed sword is something new, but I sense very relevant. He seems to be describing an angel. Not just any angel but an archangel. These powerful angels are the symbol of true courage. They've no limitations of time or space. They stand for all that is good. When you see one of them it means that God is protecting you from evil. Legend has it that Lucifer was once one of God's mighty archangels who succumbed to his dark side and fell from grace. His punishment by God was to be banished forever into the darkness. He became the Anti-Angel or Antichrist now known as the Devil, whose sole existence is to corrupt and seduce all that's good in order to steal their souls so that they can never enter the afterlife. The presence of this powerful archangel of God in this vision with the boy has to be the key. It means we're getting closer to the truth about our American spirit. What puzzles me is why this vision was shown to Sergeant Dredge? Why didn't we sense or receive any communication from the spirit world when we were in his bedroom? Did he indicate the time that this metamorphosis took place, Robyn?'

'No, he didn't. But now that you mention it he did say it wasn't long after that that the body was taken to the mortuary, which we know arrived at about ten-thirty.'

'Precisely. He just happened to be there at the crucial time. Everything comes to an end for our American spirit at ten-thirty on the first of June. He was calling for help and the vision was another clue. Now we've another presence to seek out it's even more imperative that we find this stream or waterfall. Everything is leading us to Homerville in South Carolina where our American spirit's life began.'

The clock over the fireplace chimes six times. Aunt Lizzy comes bouncing into the room, announcing that she's back and dinner will be ready in an hour, which is just enough time for me to write up my notes in my diary. Robyn makes her way to the office to prepare all the paperwork for tomorrow's trip and then to her room to pack. Jack also goes to his rooms at the top of the house to telephone some military connections he has in America. Monty makes his way into the library to finalise his preparations for tomorrow.

What dark secrets will we uncover about our American spirit? Who is he really?

My gift is already telling me that our journey to America will reveal all.

8

Secrets

We make our way through the airport looking for Sam and sure enough there she is waving. No mistaking that beautiful frame, she'd stand out anywhere, with her hourglass figure, elfin face, large cat-like eyes, and thick short black spiky hair. We hug and kiss each other like long lost sisters. Whenever we're apart it's as if a little piece of me is missing, for I've known Sam for so long that, like Monty, I can't imagine her not being in my life.

'It's great to be together again and I can't wait to get you settled into the house so we can catch up. Oh and wait till you see your transport – I've managed to wangle the use of my friend's limousine while I'm staying at her house. You know me – style and elegance is my middle name,' says Sam, excitedly, as we make our way to the limousine that even impresses Monty and Jack with its size and opulent interior.

'This has everything in it except the kitchen sink,' Monty chuckles as he helps Jack and himself to a drink from the bar.

'It feels a bit strange sitting in the back seat drinking instead of driving but I'm sure I'll adjust,' says Jack, sitting back while his eyes dart everywhere, finally ending up boring through the back of the driver's head.

We laugh and chat happily until we arrive at a large

dark-looking house in one of the richest parts of New York, which Sam has nicknamed 'Royalty Street'. Apparently her friend is the wife of the owner, who is a well renowned and respected Supreme Court Arbiter and a good friend of Sam's husband Leo, a High Court Judge back in England. We arrive at an entrance hall, which is big enough to land a plane in and are shown to our rooms by the butler.

'Makes your little estate in the country pale into insignificance, my darling,' I say jokingly as we unpack and make ourselves comfortable while proceeding to check out the most important piece of furniture, the bed.

'That's what I like, jumbo king size with plenty of room for an entire orchestra. I think we'll be fairly comfortable here, spud?' Monty quips while bouncing up and down on the bed like a teenager instead of a mature aristocrat. We make our way down to the magnificent drawing-room with its vast open fireplace dominating the centre of the room, while Sam and the others make themselves comfortable as the butler and maid dutifully serve drinks and nibbles.

'I see you've settled into the "Royalty Street" lifestyle fairly quickly then,' I joke as Monty and I make our way to the huge tapestry chairs around the open fireplace, above which is the biggest portrait I've ever seen, depicting a rather grand-looking middle-aged man dressed in all his legal regalia, sitting on what looks like a massive throne. Standing upright beside him is a rather stiff looking, much younger woman with blonde hair and a cold, detached, expressionless face. As I continue to stare at the portrait, feeling strangely uncomfortable, the odd-looking and rather frosty butler dutifully offers Monty and me some nibbles and drinks before we settle down and discuss preliminaries.

'Are your friends happy with us staying, Sam? We

wouldn't want to take liberties,' I comment, feeling rather uncomfortable in such a grand and rather cold house. Not a house that I feel has much happiness in it. All my senses tell me that the people who live here live only for themselves and not each other.

'No problem,' replies Sam. 'They're both away for the next couple of weeks so I'm effectively house sitting for them and I've told them you're coming to stay for a couple of days or so and they're absolutely OK with that.'

'Well, I'm absolutely OK with that too and could get accustomed to this lifestyle very quickly,' Robyn chips in, looking very contented in her new environment.

'We'd better formulate the next step of the TIE, team, if we're to complete our quest. What's on the agenda with regard to Mallon Enterprises here in New York, Sam, and the business partner Donald Coleman? Is there any way of getting to see him and check out the business? Also, I'm keen to find this "love-child". Any joy there?'

Sam laughs, throwing her head back in her usual nonchalant manner while balancing a drink in one hand and a cigarette in the other, a habit I keep nagging her to give up but without success.

'Impatient as ever, my dear Charity, but you've no need to worry – I've been doing a lot more digging around since we spoke last and called in a few well overdue favours. What I'm about to disclose could prove to be highly dangerous if Mallon's wife and children find out.'

'We prefer to call them the "Dark Trio",' jokes Robyn.

'As usual, my dear, you seemed to have chosen a very apt nickname,' laughs Sam as she continues. 'Well this Dark Trio are very bad people indeed and won't take kindly to us interfering in their affairs. We must move quietly and swiftly if we're to succeed and under no circumstances can we leave a trail behind us. If they discover what we're up to not only will we be in great danger but anybody that has given us information or helped us in any way will also suffer their wrath.'

'Don't worry, Sam, we'll do our best to protect your friends. What have you got for us?' Monty interrupts, hoping to reassure her.

'Firstly, I've managed to get you an appointment this afternoon with Donald Coleman at his offices here in New York. I told him that you were Mallon's psychic adviser and that you had something important to tell him about his death. That seemed to grab his attention. I also made it clear that it wouldn't be wise to inform the Dark Trio of your presence here in New York. I've also been busy with regard to Alex and Lucy Mallon's other business activities, which I've discovered are not recorded anywhere in Mallon Enterprises.'

'Do you mean Alex Mallon's guns and military weapons trafficking along with Lucy's drug smuggling activities?' Jack says, interrupting and keen to know more.

'I might have known you'd be on the case with this one, Jack. One of my contacts has put me in touch with a high ranking colonel in the Army who has joined forces with another senior officer in the Air Force. Together they've been investigating Alex and Lucy and from what I've been told they're nearly ready to bust their operations wide open and finally bring them down. Both of them are having a final secret meeting at a safe house along with a third man, who I don't know anything about but believe is a Detective Inspector in the New York Police Department. I've informed my source that Monty is involved with the British Government in Special Operations and has some useful information regarding Alex and Lucy's activities. That seemed to interest them and they're prepared to let you come along to the meeting at the safe house, which is at eight tonight, so long as you come alone and tell no one.'

Monty and Jack's faces light up. At last they'll be able to crack the case that has eluded everyone else so far. 'That's definitely a meeting I want to attend,' Monty replies, all eager and ready for action.

'I'm not happy about you going alone, honey, you don't know these people and it all sounds very tenuous. There's something about it that doesn't feel right,' I say, feeling very frightened, for my gift tells me that there's dark forces surrounding this meeting.

'Don't worry, Miss Charity. Monty won't be alone. I'll be right with him, only they won't know it. I also made a few phone calls last night to some ex-army buddies here in America. I'll get in touch with them today to see what further information I can find out about these three men,' responds Jack, eager to reassure me.

'There you are, spud, nothing to worry about. Jack and I will be fine. We do this undercover thing all the time back home, don't we, Jack?'

'Absolutely, a piece of cake,' replies Jack, trying to look calm, cool and in control.

'Just be careful, you two, and remember, nothing or no one is what they seem – the Devil has disciples everywhere,' I say, still trusting my gift, which tells me that all this information regarding Alex and Lucy Mallon seems to have surfaced very conveniently. I know Sam has many influential contacts and friends but somehow I'm not convinced that any of them would be brave enough to help her or us against the Dark Trio.

'Well, that's you two sorted. Now back to the Mallon family. What have you uncovered about the secret love-child, Sam?' I ask, keen to discover where and who she is.

'Well, I don't wish to brag but I've really excelled myself here. All the best bits of information are obtained through the rich wives circuit. You know those who lunch, shop and sleep away from home, so to speak. Anyway, one of these sleep away wives confided in me that she's seeing a very well connected bank mogul who, during their pillow talk, mentioned Mallon's other families. Now what's intriguing is that he meant more than one family.'

'What do mean, "more than one family"? Did Mallon have more than one love-child floating around?' Robyn asks, by now all ears.

'I'm not sure,' replies Sam. 'Apparently there are two separate bank accounts or trusts that Mallon set up in secret. This bank mogul is the only one who knows about them and only he has access to the accounts and operates them on behalf of Mallon. No one else at the bank knows that they even exist and her lover set them up by using an elaborate system of dummy accounts that would be impossible to trace back to Mallon. My friend thinks that Mallon had something on her lover as she's been sleeping with him for the last five years or so and he never mentioned these accounts until he heard about Mallon's death. Even now he's still afraid and continues to operate the accounts. She said that when he slipped up and told her about them he immediately went into a frenzied panic, begging her not to reveal his secret to anyone. Then she went cold, saying that he almost had a heart attack, stating that if anybody found out he would be dammed for ever. The only reason she's told me is that she now feels afraid and doesn't trust her lover. He seems to be acting strangely and is especially nervous around her, and she even thinks that he might kill her to keep his secret.'

'Did he tell her anything about the other families or the accounts so we can trace them?' I ask, feeling almost euphoric, because Sam has now confirmed what my gift of 'clear seeing' had already shown me, the existence of another family, who I sensed was connected to Mallon's past. This family I believe is the key to the boy in my

97

visions, and these two accounts will lead us not only to him, but also the other daughter, who's both Mallon's murderer and saviour at the same time.

'All she knows is that the two accounts were set up years apart,' replies Sam as she continues. 'The first account was initiated forty years ago and originated from Homerville, South Carolina. Now, he didn't tell her as much but my friend got the impression that he also came from there, which leads me to believe he knew Mallon when he was a young man. Her lover is about the same age and has a slight Southern accent. The other account was instigated twenty years ago here in New York.'

'So, again we've a connection with the town Homerville. We're constantly being drawn towards this place. But first we need to gain access to the accounts so that we can find the daughter and other families, but without the lover knowing otherwise it could jeopardise your friend's life,' I say, anxious to protect Sam's friend but at the same time eager to discover who the beneficiaries of these secret accounts might be.

'Does your friend ever meet her lover in his home, as he more than likely keeps the information about the accounts locked away there? It would be too risky for him to keep it at the bank,' enquires Jack, with Monty nodding in agreement.

'Yes she does. His wife spends long weekends away at her family's estate; they've been married for over twenty years but basically lead separate lives. So whenever either his wife or my friend's husband is away they meet up; sometimes at his house and other times at a small apartment they keep solely for their rendezvous.'

'We need to gain access to his house so I'll need a plan of the security system plus the location and combination of his safe. Can your friend get hold of this for us without compromising herself, plus arrange for him to meet her at their apartment, say this weekend, so that Monty and I can do a spot of night work?'

'You're asking a lot, Jack. I'm not sure she can or would be willing to do any of that. It's too risky. What if he finds out?'

'Don't worry, Sam,' Monty replies. 'Jack and I are experts at night work. We just need to gain access, find the safe and copy the relevant data. Her lover will never even know that we've been in the house.'

Sam sits pondering for a few moments, wondering whether she's the right to ask such a dangerous favour of her friend. I share her concerns but also feel that if we could get her friend to help us, in the long term it would be to her benefit. For if we solve this mystery then it could also mean removing any threat that her lover may have on her.

'I know you are worried, Sam, but if you could get your friend to help us then we can help her in return, as it sounds to me like she would prefer to be free of this relationship rather than living in constant fear,' I say, trying to both comfort and reassure her at the same time.

'You're right about her living in constant fear, and I think she would help if it meant she could feel safe again. I'll be meeting her for lunch today so will put it to her then,' Sam replies, still feeling protective towards her friend, but trusting in the RING to do the right thing.

'What about me? Monty and Jack have their undercover stuff to do and Sam's lunching, while Charity's meeting the business partner. What's left for me?' says Robyn, feeling a bit dejected and left out.

'I need you to come with me to Mallon Enterprises, because while I'm chatting to Donald Coleman you can do a bit of sleuthing yourself. Be subtle though, we don't want the staff reporting back to the Dark Trio that we've been there,' I say, knowing how sensitive Robyn can be at times.

'Don't worry. You can rely on me. Discretion is my middle name and it's lucky that my new mobile phone has a camera in it, which might come in handy,' Robyn replies, now a lot chirpier that she's been given the job of sleuthing.

The rest of us all look at each other and smile at Robyn's sudden transformation.

'Oh stop making fun of me, you lot, we're the RING. All for one and one for all – the Psychic Musketeers and woe betide anybody who stands in our way,' Robyn says, raising her hand in the air with clenched fist, making light of the situation. Then we all join in the fun as we raise our hands, shouting, 'Evil beware, the Psychic Musketeers are here', while we laugh nervously to hide our own secret fears. For underneath, all of us are worried as so many things could go wrong. Monty and Jack could be entering a trap tonight at the safe house. Sam's friend may panic and instead of helping us, tell her lover everything in the hope that he won't harm her. Robyn and I could come unstuck when we meet Donald Coleman at Mallon Enterprises. If Monty and Jack survive tonight and Sam's friend comes through with the goods, will they get away with the night work this weekend? Will the Dark Trio discover we're here and call upon their Master for help? We've only been in town a few hours and already I can feel my heart beating faster and my blood racing with that lethal cocktail of excitement and danger.

'Right everybody, let's synchronise our watches and define our plan,' I say, trying to appear calm and in control, while underneath shaking with trepidation at what dark forces are about to descend upon us.

'You look so cute when you talk tough and your little face crinkles up, spud,' Monty says, jokingly, while helping

100

himself to some more nibbles, grinning and winking at me. Then we go over everything again to make sure that nothing has been missed before we set off on our separate assignments.

Robyn and I set off for our meeting with Donald Coleman. Sam goes off to meet her friend for lunch and Monty and Jack make preparations for their meeting at the safe house tonight. We arrive at Mallon Enterprises, a tall glass building that eclipses the entire street, and enter the huge reception area with its marble floors, cascading waterfall in the centre and glass lifts. We make our way to the grand marble reception desk, noticing that the dark-suited security guards seem to be everywhere.

'My name is Charity Holmes and we've an appointment with Donald Coleman.'

If looks could kill, Robyn and I would be dead right now. After the iceberg receptionist checks us out she then points to the third lift, stating that we should press the penthouse button. She indicates to the dark suits to let us pass and within seconds Robyn and I are making our way up in the glass lifts to the penthouse. The doors open and we're greeted by two further dark suits and shown into a suite of rooms. We make our way through two rooms, both decorated and furnished in leather and dark wood with yet more iceberg receptionists and dark suits in each room. Finally we are shown into a huge room with a massive dark wooden circular desk in the centre, which seems to be the pivotal point of the room. In the background is a wall of glass, that, as we draw closer, gives the impression that you're viewing the world from a place of supreme power. Seated in the centre is Donald Coleman with more dark suits flanked on either side of him. As we draw closer I see exactly the man

Sam described, for his outside persona portrays the man within. The aura emanating from him is dull and lifeless, depicting a sad lonely man in his mid-fifties with short, slightly balding grey hair. His face is sallow with deep-set, almost colourless eyes surrounded by lines. It is a face that betrays the shallow life he's led. As we sit down I notice that our chairs are much lower than his, giving him the advantage of superiority over whoever is before him.

'I believe my appointment was with a Miss Charity Holmes alone. There was no mention of another person,' he says in a smug Southern American drawl, which hasn't the power behind it that Mallon's voice had during his materialisation. No wonder he has so many suits around him, I think to myself, for the man is but an empty shell, devoid of any hope or life.

'You're absolutely right, Mr Coleman, but Robyn is my personal assistant and completely trustworthy.'

He looks at Robyn and me in a shifty manner with shaky hands that he tries to hide by clutching them tightly on top of the table.

'I understand that you were Stephen's psychic adviser, whatever that is, and that you've some important information about his death,' he says, mockingly.

'That's right, but what I've got to say is for your ears only,' I say, glancing over at the suits standing either side, indicating that it wouldn't be to his advantage for them to listen in. As I sensed, he is a man who needs the reassurance of his entourage around him, but his curiosity, or maybe fear, takes over and he indicates to the suits that the room be cleared. This is Robyn's signal to make up an excuse to leave the room in the hope that she can do a bit of sleuthing.

'I'm afraid I need to use the bathroom,' Robyn says, squirming convincingly in her chair.

102

Coleman scowls at Robyn, indicating his annoyance, and then points the way to the bathroom, which is back through one of the rooms we came in from. That was it, she was off, leaving me to deal with him. Hmm, how best to tackle this? I need to rattle his cage a bit to see what happens. I need to know if he's in collusion with the Dark Trio and what he gains from Mallon's death. I think I'll just go straight for the jugular, as my 'clear seeing' tells me that he's more worried about Alex Mallon taking over the business than his partner being dead.

'It was my understanding that you managed the South Carolina office along with Stephen Mallon, while his son Alex managed the New York one. Does your presence here mean that you'll be taking over things or are you just overseeing while his family are in England?'

I can see him physically sweating and know that I have touched a nerve, so I continue. 'Or perhaps now that your partner is no longer in the mortal world, his wife will no doubt inherit the business, making you a much smaller shareholder. With Nancy inheriting the other forty per cent of her husband's shares, she would own sixty-five per cent of the company. Enough I would have thought to effect a take-over and put Alex and Lucy in charge. Not a position that would sit comfortably with you I would think, for I doubt if Alex Mallon is the type that needs or wants a partner.' That certainly hits a nerve.

'I thought that you had some information for me regarding Stephen's death. Anything else regarding my or the family's position within Mallon Enterprises is none of your business. I don't think Mrs Mallon or her children will be too pleased to hear that you've been digging about in their affairs, while their father is barely cold in his grave. What exactly do you know about Stephen and how do you come to know him? I've never heard him mention you before.'

His reaction to my questions and his whole demeanour indicate to me that he's not in collusion with the Dark Trio. His presence here and the army of dark suits tells me the opposite – that he's afraid and needs protection. While Mallon was alive he was safe. Although they didn't get along, there was a kind of truce between them with regard to the shares in the company and their partnership. Now that he's dead this leaves Donald Coleman in a very perilous position. For I'm sure Alex Mallon, with the help of his Master will find a way to get hold of Donald Coleman's remaining shares.

'His spirit visited me, seeking my help. I'm now seeking the truth on his behalf.'

He laughs but in a fearful way. For although I sense he doesn't quite know whether to believe me or not, my gift of 'clear seeing' shows me that he's surrounded by an evil presence.

'What do mean, "Seeking the truth"? What else did he tell you when his so-called spirit visited you?' he asks, but this time the laughter has stopped and is replaced by a more frightened tone.

'Stephen Mallon was a man with a dark secret. He wasn't what he seemed. He came into the world by other means. He was born forty years ago not sixty. I'm seeking the secret of his previous life. His soul will be dammed forever unless I can unlock his secret and give him redemption. His children are also not what they appear – they have dark souls and will stop at nothing to achieve their ambitions. I know they're not responsible for their father's death, as that was just a matter of timing, for if he hadn't been murdered by another they would've killed him on the first of June. I believe the person who did murder him did so out of love, which gave his spirit the opportunity to seek me out and ask for my help. I'm now in search of his murderer, for her life is in danger along with yours. Believe me when I say you are within the jaws of the darkest of evils. Help me to unlock Stephen Mallon's past and I will help you against the forces of darkness; the disciples of this dark force are Alex and Lucy Mallon.'

He listens not with disbelief but knowing that what I say is true. I sense he is waiting for something terrible to happen to him. He is a man living in constant fear.

'I could tell everything you've told me to Nancy or Alex but for some reason I trust you. I never got along with Stephen for reasons that you no doubt already know. But his children are something else. Just being in their presence makes me feel cold. I could never put my finger on why but your description of them explains all. They have a coldness and darkness about them that touches everything and everyone they come into contact with. I'm not sure what you are seeking from me but I'll help you if I can. Not for Stephen's sake, for he deserves his fate, but for myself, as I know that time is running out for me. They want me out of the way and I don't know how to stop them. As you see, I'm surrounded by an army, yet I know they can't protect me. But I'm puzzled. Why are you so sure they would have killed their own father on the first of June?'

'Because that was the date forty years ago that Stephen Mallon was reborn, when as a young man of twenty he signed a contract with the Devil and in return was promised all his desires. To enter into this contract he had to take another soul and the price he pays is that the Devil claims his soul on that date. Alex and Lucy are the Devil's disciples, here to do their Master's bidding, which is to kill their father on the precise date and time that the contract is due, and in return their Master must have promised them their ultimate desires. But Mallon was murdered before they could complete their end of

105

the contract. They'll now use any means necessary to make sure their father's soul is claimed by their Master on the agreed date. I have until that time to save him otherwise his soul will be lost forever. From what I've learnt about him so far, you're probably right in saying he deserves his fate. But there's another soul within him that needs saving; the one he stole. I need to find that other soul, because until I do, the person it belongs to will also be taken by the Devil. No one deserves that fate. I also need to find his killer, who I know to be his love-child, otherwise her fate will be the same as her father's. Will you help me?'

There's a long pause and I see for the first time another side to Donald Coleman. Not the shallow man he has become, but the man I sense he was many years ago.

'There was always a part of Stephen I could never quite understand. He had a coldness and ruthlessness about him that made you afraid of him, yet sometimes he seemed to be struggling within himself as if he was in torment. I could never quantify it before but now I can. Two souls struggling within the one body, the darker one always winning yet never really free of the other. I guess he's been fighting demons for the last forty years and in a strange sort of way meeting you and hearing about Stephen has released me. For I always thought he'd stolen my life but it looks like he's paid a higher price than me for his.'

At that moment Robyn returns and as she sits down Coleman continues. 'There have been rumours for years that Stephen had a love-child but no one has been able to trace her or her mother. For as long as I've known him I've never seen him with another woman. If he had a lover he kept her well hidden. He had plenty of women over the years but they meant nothing to him yet I felt that there was someone he did care about. It would have been about twenty years ago back home in Church Town. For a while he seemed a changed man, almost human again. Maybe the daughter and mother you're seeking are there. I've tried to find them and I know Nancy has been searching for years. Wherever they are he kept them well hidden, for Church Town is like all small Southern American towns – everyone knows everybody's business. There is one thing. Every few weeks he would disappear for a few days. He'd never say where he went or why. Somehow he always managed to cover his tracks so that Nancy, Alex, Lucy or I couldn't discover what his secret was. I always felt he was visiting his other love, maybe this is the woman you're seeking?'

Robyn and I glance at each other. The name Church Town seemed rather ironic considering that its most powerful residents were the Devil's disciples. We also know that we have to go there.

'We need to go to Church Town. Can you help us?' I ask anxiously. 'Also, we need to find a town called Homerville. Do you know of it and how far is it from Church Town? We believe that's where Mallon originally came from.' Suddenly he looks startled, and immediately I sense he knows more than he is telling.

'I know of the town Homerville. It's about one hundred and twenty miles further South of Church Town. I've never been there, nor have any desire to. People who've been there say it's a dark town where its people are unfriendly and don't take kindly to strangers. There was talk that Stephen murdered a man there who he worked for, but it was never proven. It's rumoured that the town sheriff helped him cover it up. Shortly after that Stephen rapidly gained influence and power over the town with the sheriff being his chief henchman. You go there at great risk, for although Stephen came to Church Town twenty-five years ago, he still owned Homerville and the town sheriff. As for Church Town, the Mallons own that as well and everyone in it. Even though Stephen is dead, the Mallons' power continues through his children. No one will help you in either town.'

'There must be something you can do? Remember, if you help us find the truth we may be able to help you against Alex and Lucy,' I say softly, convinced that he's as much a victim as the lost soul of Mallon.

'There is a man. His name is David Shield. He used to be the town vicar. He was a good man, who cared for his people, but when Stephen arrived on the scene everything changed and the town and its people became darker and greed took over. David fought for years against Stephen's influence but without success. He left the church about ten years ago and now lives in an old run-down house outside the town in the backwoods. He's a shadow of the man he once was. The people who used to look up to him now mock and laugh at him. He makes a living of sorts by selling sketches and paintings. He knows things about Stephen that I'm sure no one else does and I suspect he knows about his lover and the child. Nancy, Alex and Lucy have tried everything to get the information from him, but for some reason, though he's a broken man, he remains unafraid of them, and they haven't been able to destroy him completely. If anybody can help you, David can.'

'Can you contact him?' I ask, knowing that this David Shield will lead us not only to Mallon's love-child, but also to the boy in my vision and his other family.

'I'll do my best, but can promise nothing.'

I give him my mobile phone number and shake his hand while looking deep into his eyes. Gone is the shallow man I saw when we entered the room, replaced by the real Donald Coleman, a good man who didn't have the strength within him to fight the dark forces that came into his life, namely Stephen Mallon and his children. With that, Robyn and I leave, feeling relieved that we never have to enter this cold and soulless building again.

'Did you discover anything while you were out of the room?' I ask as we make our way back to the house.

'No, it was impossible. The room was full of iceberg receptionists and dark suits, plus there were surveillance cameras everywhere, even in the ladies' room. But I did overhear the receptionist speaking on the phone and I'm almost certain she was talking to Alex Mallon. I'm afraid we may have visitors fairly soon.'

'Then we'd better be prepared for them. Remember, God protects the good and destroys the evil. We've his protection and must trust in that,' I say as we arrive back at the house, hoping that 'Himself' as Aunt Lizzy likes to call him is listening to me. We make our way into the drawing-room where Monty, Jack and Sam are settled in their chosen chairs with drinks and nibbles.

'So the RING is united again,' jokes Monty as he walks towards me exuding that powerful combination of magnetism and tenderness that I find so irresistible as he kisses me intensely on my lips, which even after all these years still ignites my whole being.

Thirty minutes later, as we move into the dining-room, we continue to discuss our day over dinner, while planning the next step of the TIE. Robyn and I run through our meeting with Donald Coleman, while Sam reports that her friend is willing to help us and hopes to have all the information about her lover's house that Monty and Jack need for their night work before the weekend; two days from now. Then Monty and Jack report that they've made preparations for tonight's meeting, Jack stating that he's arranged for a couple of ex-army buddies to join them.

Monty did some checking on the high-ranking colonel in the Army and the other senior officer in the Air Force. His sources at the British Secret Service confirm that they are, as far as they know, honourable and fair men. However he was unable to uncover much about the other detective inspector in the New York Police Force. Monty's contact stated that there was no hard evidence to say he was corrupt, but that he has a reputation as a rather cold, ignoble man, and that anyone dealing with him should be extra cautious. Listening to Monty and Jack's report, my gift of 'clear seeing' still warns me that they're entering a trap, but I know that they won't be dissuaded from going tonight and so decide to help them in the only way I know how.

'I know I can't persuade you two not to go tonight so I'll keep an eye on you both through the ancient tarot and crystal,' I announce.

Monty and Jack smile but I sense they're glad that I shall be watching over them. Even such strong men sometimes need the power of 'clear seeing' behind them. After dinner Monty and Jack make final preparations to leave for their meeting, while Sam and Robyn make their way to their rooms to change and get ready for my reading tonight. Then Monty and I spend the last few minutes together alone, as we always do, when he's about to embark on an operation with Jack.

Finally, we all touch rings before Monty and Jack set off into the night.

9

The Power of Three

As soon as they've left I return to my room to prepare
for my reading: perform the chakras and collect my crystal
ball and ancient tarot cards, which I always carry with
me wherever I journey. At home I keep them wrapped
in silk in wooden boxes, but when travelling I've special
velvet pouches with silk lining to protect them (retain
their energy), plus my velvet casting cloth. I return to
the drawing-room and move a small round table from
near the fireplace into the centre of the room, placing
three chairs around it, then wrap my velvet casting cloth
over the table. I carefully remove my crystal ball from
its protective velvet pouch and place it in the centre of
the table, finally repeating the same ritual with my ancient
tarot cards, as I place them on the side of the table.
There are 78 cards in the tarot, which are split into two
decks. One deck has 22 cards and is called the Major
Arcana and the other has 56 cards called the Minor
Arcana, but tonight I'll only use the Major Arcana. Through
the tarot and crystal ball I will use my gift of 'clear
seeing' to seek out and find those who are the Devil's
disciples. As Sam and Robyn enter the room I turn the
lights off, then the three of us sit around the table. Sam
doesn't have the gift but her love for Monty and Jack
will be a powerful energy that I can channel and use.

Robyn's love combined with her gift completes the circle required to form the Power of Three. This is a powerful force, which if channelled together as one will seek out and destroy the dark forces that would harm our loved ones. Lastly I perform the final (but most essential) ritual as I place an outer circle of lighted scented candles around the table forming a protective seal that will keep out the evil spirits that would try to destroy us. Now we're ready for the reading to begin...

I ask Sam to close her eyes and empty her mind and think only of her love for Monty and Jack, while Robyn and I close our eyes and silently reaffirm the chakras. As I begin to feel their energy flow within me I take the Major Arcana cards and shuffle them before passing them on to Robyn and then Sam to do the same, finally returning to me to complete the circle. Now the three of us have passed all our energies into the cards. I take four cards from the deck and place them face down on the table in a circle around the crystal ball. I turn the cards one by one to reveal their message.

Card One: The Moon; a warning card; beware.
(I see danger. Must be on one's guard. Deception. A man with two faces.)
Card Two: The Tower; shock; fear.
(I see shattered images. A false illusion. The sudden realisation of truth.)
Card Three: The Devil; the beast; evil.
(I see the dark side. Avarice, greed and power. The beast within us.)
Card Four: Death; loss; ending.
(I see leaving something behind. Possession. The End.)

112

The message I see in these cards shows a man who's not what he seems. He hides behind a false face. He has left all goodness behind him with the promise of great power and riches. He's succumbed to the beast within and given his soul over to the dark side. There's no going back for him. His fate is sealed. He brings death and destruction with him. My heart beats faster and my whole body shakes with panic and fear. For now I know that one of the three men that Monty meets tonight comes with a false face. He's the Devil's disciple and comes to destroy. I look at Robyn and sense her fear and know she sees it too. Sam sees our fear and asks, 'What do you see? I'm afraid.'

'I see the Devil's disciple who brings death. We must stop him. We must use the Power of Three through the crystal to seek him out and destroy,' I say, knowing that time is running out, for the clock on the wall reads 7.55 p.m.

'I need to channel all our energies together as one. We three must make our minds as one thought then I can use my power of "clear seeing" through the crystal to find the Devil's disciple. Close your minds now. Clear your thoughts and think only of Monty and Jack. Picture them in your mind's eye and feel their presence. Feel their heartbeat. Hear their voices. See their bodies. Let them into your mind's eye. Picture them now.'

Then I feel it, intensifying heat racing through my body, until my head and hands feel as if they're on fire. I place my hands on the crystal, channelling the heat from me into it and as the heat goes deep into the crystal it becomes alive. A flame appears in the centre, which begins to grow bigger and bigger until the whole crystal becomes luminous. Then the vision appears.

We see Jack and two men hiding in bushes outside a large house. They're talking to each other with concealed

113

two-way radios with their faces painted black and holding guns. We see Monty walking into a room with three other men. The room is dark as the windows are sealed with wooden boards. There are white sheets over the furniture. There's only one light in the room but it's dull so difficult to see clearly. The men are shadowy figures so we can't see their faces but I can see that they have guns. They search Monty and take his gun but find no hidden microphone. Where has he hidden it? How will Jack hear to protect him? Jack can't see him as the windows are boarded. How will he see to protect him? I feel an overwhelming sense of helplessness and know something terrible is about to happen. The men talk but we can't hear what they're saying, because the crystal shows only visions. Then one man begins to move away, leaving Monty and the other two in the centre of the room. He moves further and further into the background, almost disappearing into the shadows of the walls. Monty and the other two suddenly notice that he's not there and turn to find him. We see Monty calling his name but can't hear him. He calls it again and I know something is wrong. We see Jack and the two men running out of the bushes towards the house. He must know Monty's in trouble. There must be a hidden microphone on him somewhere. Jack and the two men rush towards the house but I fear they won't make it in time.

Then he returns, the third man; from out of the shadows he 'floats' towards Monty and the other two men with his body transforming as he moves. He grows bigger and bigger until he towers over them. As he grows the room shrinks and becomes darker as the boards on the windows and the door change to stone, making the whole room impenetrable. We see Jack and his men outside unable to enter as Monty and the two men inside are unable to get out. They're unable to communicate with each other,

114

with Monty trapped inside and Jack outside. The room is suddenly aflame with a huge towering beast, a horned reptile whose entire scaly body is blood red. It has a long red tongue and tail with sharp red claws and flashing Satanic red eyes. Its teeth are pointed and dripping with blood, ready to devour its victims, while lashing its tail from side to side, knocking one of the men to the ground. Then it swoops down for the kill. Monty and the other man try to save him but their guns are useless against such a beast as it swings its massive head and opens its jaws, letting out the flames of Hell. They cower back into the walls as the beast devours its prey and within seconds the man on the floor is no more.

The three of us watch in despair, for there's no way out. They can't fight this beast. Soon Monty and the other man will be gone; lost forever. I have but seconds to save them, but how? I must think. How from outside the crystal can I enter and destroy this flaming beast? Then it comes to me. COLD. I will freeze it to death. Quickly, I tell Robyn and Sam to close their minds and clear their thoughts. Concentrate your mind's eye and think ICE. Concentrate on solid cold ice. See icebergs. See frozen lakes. Feel the cold as it penetrates your body. You're frozen with the cold. Your whole body is dying from the cold. Then I feel it: a chilling feverish cold racing through my body. My hands become blue and frozen to the point of stiffness. I feel the cold running through my fingers into the crystal. I look into it and see the beast slithering towards Monty, ready to swallow him up within his flames. He's unable to move and I see him stare into its eyes, waiting for the end.

I concentrate and draw on my power within and feel its force surge through me as my fingers become like icicles penetrating through the crystal into the flaming vision within. The whole crystal becomes one big circle of ice.

115

The room freezes and transforms itself into a large cavern of ice, becoming so cold we can see Monty's breath evaporate into the air. There's a clear blue mist forming all around them, which moves towards the beast, causing its flames to freeze within its huge jaws, forming large stalactites. Its teeth crack and break, dissolving into the floor, which has become one clear sheet of ice. Its claws become embedded in the ice and it's unable to move. It struggles relentlessly, trying to free its claws from beneath the frozen floor. The more it struggles the deeper it sinks with its scaly body now frozen white with icicles and stalactites. The beast swings its frozen tail, trying to lash out towards the men who are almost mummified with ice, unable to move. I have but seconds to act otherwise Monty and the other man will most certainly die from the cold.

I move closer towards the crystal, while breathing in as deep as I dare, concentrating all my power, then I breathe out into the crystal, directly onto the beast, forming a torrent of frozen ice that encases it completely. Suddenly it shatters into a thousand pieces that eclipses the whole room and instantly it's no more. Within seconds light and warmth return, with Monty and the other man cold, shaken and wet but very much alive. Jack and his men burst into the room only to find two rather soggy looking comrades. Just at that moment the vision begins to disappear, and as it fades away, I see Monty look up and smile, knowing that tonight the Power of Three were his guardian angels. The three of us sit back in our chairs, our bodies completely drained of their energies as my head pounds with the most horrendous migraine, which I often get when using my powers to their fullest. We look at each other, exhausted, yet overwhelmed with relief that Monty and Jack are safe. Robyn and Sam make their way to the fire, helping themselves to a well-earned drink from the cabinet on *en route*. I sit quietly for a few moments, performing my chakras in order to close my body and mind to the spirit world. Slowly my head begins to clear and my migraine disappears and I join Robyn and Sam on the couch by the fire feeling a warm glow of both relief and tiredness. Within minutes I find myself drifting into a deep sleep, comforted by the thought that my Monty will soon return.

I hear a distant voice echoing in the background and feel a large, strong hand tenderly shaking me with the words, 'Wake up, my darling' gently drifting into my mind as I open my eyes to see those big soft brown eyes staring down on me. I feel his tender kiss on my cheek and his soft words again in my ear, 'Come, my darling, time to share that sleep', as we make our way to the bedroom. Soon I'm drifting back into the most wonderful deep sleep, feeling safe and secure as Monty gently puts his strong arms around me.

At the breakfast table the five of us sit happily chatting, continuing to plan the next step in the TIE, but silently feeling an overwhelming sense of relief that the beast is dead.

'Did you discover anything last night?' asks Robyn, as she tucks into another helping of scrambled eggs and toast. How she manages to eat so much and stay so slim has always been a mystery to me especially as the rest of our family gain weight just breathing air.

'You mean you didn't see anything in the crystal while you were saving me from the beast?' quips Monty, grinning away, while Jack tucks into his second breakfast. It must be the New York air, as everyone seems to have the appetite of a horse this morning.

'Which one of the men was the beast? Which one died? What about the other man left?' Who was he and did you find anything out from him?, I ask while munching away at my two thin slices of toast.

'So many questions and not enough answers,' Monty replies, pouring himself yet another cup of black coffee. 'The beast was the New York detective and the man who died an Air Force captain. The remaining man was Colonel Sharpe. He was working with the Air Force captain, compiling a case against Alex and Lucy Mallon. The New York detective, alias the beast, contacted them only yesterday, stating that he'd vital information regarding Mallon Enterprises. When questioned about how he knew of their investigation he informed them that there was a leak in their organisation, but it was too dangerous to speak on the phone and needed to meet them in person. When I arrived it was clear that something was wrong. Once they searched me and took my gun the detective started moving away from the group. Colonel Sharpe said afterwards that nothing was disclosed before I arrived and then the beast appeared. Now that the captain and the detective are both dead any knowledge dies with them. The investigation into the Mallons' activities is again tainted and so once again they escape justice.'

'It was definitely a trap set by the Dark Trio. Who's the contact who told you about the meeting last night, Sam, as it's a sure bet that they're probably another disciple and in collusion with the Dark Trio?' I ask, knowing that the answer will cause Sam great pain. Sam's face shows her anguish for she is now faced with the terrible reality that one of her friends has used her to try and destroy Monty and Jack.

'I can't believe that she'd do this terrible thing. I've known her for years. We've shared so many intimate secrets. I thought she was a good and loyal friend. I find it difficult to understand why she would betray me so.'

We all sit silently for a few moments, feeling Sam's pain. Friendship is a bond that transcends all things and is the essence of who we are. Betrayal of a friendship

118

destroys a piece of your soul. It breaks and shatters your heart and the pieces can never truly be mended. Betrayal is the cruellest crime.

'Catherine Davenport, my friend for the past fifteen years and wife to Leo's best friend Michael, the Supreme Court Arbiter and owner of this house. She's the betrayer we seek,' Sam replies, desperately trying to hold back her tears.

Again the silence between us speaks volumes. Now I know why I felt such coldness in this house, as my gift of 'clear seeing' never fails me. I sensed the moment we entered that the man and woman in the portrait lived only for themselves. I wish with all my being that I were wrong, because to see the pain of betrayal etched across Sam's face breaks my heart.

'We've probably been under surveillance since we arrived. We must keep our own counsel and plan our next move very carefully. We know what we must do,' says Monty, but not in words.

From this point on we communicate in silence by using the ancient art of sign language. While in the house no words pass our lips but every word is translated and understood. We sign to each that the staff can no longer be trusted. It's also agreed that we alter our plans for tomorrow night. While Sam's friend is entertaining her lover at their apartment all of us will break into his house.

Jack disables the alarm and Monty opens the door using his set of skeleton keys, while Sam, Robyn and I follow close behind with the plans of the house and hidden safe. We make our way towards the library and look for a hidden panel within the bookcase and sure enough it's there half way down the bookcase, cleverly disguised as books. We press the third book and the secret panel

119

opens revealing a large safe, and we quickly search for information that could reveal the two secret accounts. Finally we find a CD-R compact disc with the letters SM on it.

'This has to be it. SM must mean Stephen Mallon. Now we need a computer to check it out,' whispers Monty as he looks around the room.

Then we spot a laptop just inside the top drawer of the desk by the window. Quickly, while Sam and Robyn keep a watchful guard, Monty, Jack and I start to set up the laptop with the first obstacle being a password. We try several combinations without success, as Sam's friend wasn't able to obtain this information without drawing suspicion.

'We'll never crack this. We could be here all night,' mumbles Jack, as he grows increasingly frustrated.

'We just need to concentrate. Most people use passwords that are associated with someone or something close to them. Now what would be close to this man?' I say, looking around the room, taking in the overstated opulence and splendour of the house we've just broken into. Then it hits me like a bolt of lightning: MONEY. I type the word MONEY, but it fails and I begin to feel Jack's frustration when suddenly I realise that the caps lock is on. I take it off, type it in again in lower case, and sure enough we're in. We place the disc into the computer and there they are: two files. One named CM and the other AKC.

We open the first file marked CM and there she is, Charlotte Mallon, aged 20 years and living here in New York with one bank account opened up 20 years ago, which she receives an allowance from each month. There's no mother and no other information, but at last we know who and where she is.

We open the second, marked AKC and sure enough

there they are: two names. Abraham Colby aged 52 years and Kane Colby aged 56, each with bank accounts opened 40 years ago, and, like Charlotte, receiving monies every month sent to an address in Summer Town, South Carolina, the other secret family and the key to Mallon's past. Quickly I copy the information and place the disc back in the safe as we carefully make our way out of the house, switching the alarm back on.

On the way back to the house, while Jack drives the huge limousine, we plan our next move. Tomorrow Robyn and I will visit the daughter Charlotte while Sam checks out her friends Catherine and Michael Davenport, our absent malevolent hosts. Monty and Jack shall use their contacts to see what they can uncover about Abraham and Kane Colby. I check my mobile to see if Donald Coleman has contacted me with details of David Shield, the ex-vicar from Church Town, but there are no messages. Finally we arrive back at the Davenport mansion and make our way into the drawing-room, where I immediately sense that there's something wrong. I look up at the portrait of Sam's friends and know instantly that we must leave this house if we're to survive. I glance over at Robyn and see she senses it too. This house has a darkness about it that transcends any human feeling, and the longer I stay in it the more I feel it. I sign to the others, telling them that we must leave soon. They agree. As we sit and help ourselves to drinks, the butler enters and in his usual detached, slightly sinister manner informs us that dinner will be in 30 minutes. Definitely not one of your warmer human beings, I think to myself, as my mobile rings. It's Aunt Lizzy.

'How's my darling doing then?' she says.

'Just fine, Lizzy. What's happening at your end?'

'The Dark Trio is on the move. My contact at the hotel said they left this morning after receiving a call from New York.'

'Then we'd better be one step ahead,' I reply, indicating to the others in sign language. 'What's happening with Chief Inspector Cranky, any developments there?'

'Andy, your sniffing friend from the mortuary telephoned to say that the Dark Trio tried to remove their father's body, but the Chief Inspector stopped them. His twitching sidekick Sergeant Dredge then telephoned to speak to Robyn. I didn't tell him where she was but said I would pass along any messages. He said that they couldn't detain the Dark Trio without further evidence and still haven't found the killer or murder weapon. The Chief Inspector is also after you. Be very careful, my darling. I'll be praying for yah and the others.'

Suddenly my mobile goes dead and I have one of my 'flashing visions'. Sometimes my psychic powers are so strong that I get an instant vision, a premonition of something dramatic that has just happened or is about to happen. I've no control over these visions, which nearly always show tragedy. I call them 'flashing visions' because I don't seek them nor want them. They flash into my mind's eye, showing me pictures of events that I can't always understand, but must try to unravel. I don't seek these visions, because if I can't solve them they become real. Imagine seeing something terrible that you might be able to stop if given enough time. Then imagine how you'd feel if time runs out and your vision becomes reality. These visions are the cruellest of burdens to carry.

Suddenly I see Donald Coleman in his office sitting at his desk dialling a number on his telephone; it's my mobile. Then I see Alex and Lucy Mallon enter the room as he looks up and they stare directly at him. I see their eyes; they're the colour of blood. They join hands, as

122

together they transfix Donald Coleman with their eyes. He begins to struggle and holds his chest and I feel this terrible pain as his heart beats faster and faster until it's about to burst. He tries to stand, stretching his hand out to plead with them as they stand there emotionless, continuing to stare with those blood-red eyes, still holding hands and smiling; a callous, evil smile. Within seconds he falls to the floor, his heart no longer beating. The life has been crushed out of him. Then the vision is gone and my mobile rings again. Even before I answer I know who it is and what the message will be. My heart sinks, for my 'flashing vision' has become real. I hear the voice; that empty, dark, soulless voice.

'Enjoy your vision, Charity? I hope it was real enough for you. Poor Donald, such a spineless little man. Oh, and yes, I've a message for you. "Your father is waiting for you".'

There's a transcendental silence between us with his last words cutting through my heart and soul like a sword wielded by a knight upon his victim. Then he says, 'Lucy and I look forward to seeing you very soon.'

10

New Beginnings

Those fateful words fill me with animus. Only the mention of my father brings about this terrible emotion within me. I say this with great sorrow. How can a man I've never known have such a profound effect on me? He died before I was born. I never knew him yet the very mention of him destroys any good that I feel. When I was growing up as a child his name was never spoken. It's as if he never existed. If I asked questions they were never answered. Eventually I stopped asking. My beloved Ma never spoke of him except just before she died. I asked her who my father was, to which she replied, sorrowfully, 'He gave himself over to the dark side and is no longer.'

Until this day I know nothing of him and have deliberately chosen not to seek him out. My whole being tells me that should I ever find him part of me would die. I'm afraid of nothing, yet whenever my father is mentioned I have the darkest of thoughts and become afraid. One day I'll have to face that fear and maybe then I'll know who I really am. Perhaps this is why I'm so drawn to Charlotte Mallon, our American spirit's love-child and murderer. For in her I see myself, the daughter with love and goodness in her soul, yet damaged by a father who's given himself over to the dark side. Could this be why

I've been chosen? Did Stephen Mallon know my father? Will my fate be the same as Charlotte Mallon's or is my father already lost forever to the 'dark life'?

'What's the matter, spud, you look like a ghost?' Monty whispers, holding me tightly, trying to calm my shaking body. In sign I reply.

'I've had a "flashing vision" with the Dark Trio and Donald Coleman. He's dead. They destroyed him. We're next. We must move quickly and leave this house immediately. There's no time to waste. We need to find David Shield, the man Donald Coleman was telephoning me about when they killed him. He must have knowledge that would destroy them. We need to go to Church Town and find him, but not before we talk to Charlotte Mallon.'

I don't tell them about my father. Somehow I can't bring myself to talk about him, even to my beloved Monty.

'Right then, we'll leave tonight,' replies Monty in sign and continues, 'Robyn, can you sort out the flights for South Carolina and car hire, first stop Church Town. We don't have time to do any further investigations so we'll just have to hope this David Shield can help us. We'll eat dinner as normal, pack and leave, checking out Charlotte Mallon on the way to the airport. Sam, don't contact your friends, our illustrious hosts the Davenports. We can no longer trust them.'

Within the hour we've eaten dinner, packed, and Robyn has arranged the flights and car hire using her mobile, while standing in the garden so the staff can't overhear. Monty and I make polite conversation with the butler, pretending that we're all going out for the evening, while the others secretly pack our belongings into the limousine.

125

As we drive off I look back through the fog and mist of the night at the Davenport Mansion, which now shows its true nature; a dark and gloomy Gothic building with an almost supernatural entity to it.

'Here we are, Charlotte Mallon's apartment and the lights are on,' says Jack, as we park in a side road just out of view of the apartment.

'I don't think all five of us should descend on her at once. My gift tells me she'll respond to me if I'm alone,' I say, suddenly feeling vulnerable and excited at the same time.

'No way are you going in there alone, spud. If, as you suspect, she's murdered her father then there's nothing to stop her doing it again. We don't know anything about her. She could be just like her other siblings Alex and Lucy, murderous and treacherous and not the loving daughter who you feel killed her father to save his soul,' replies Monty in his sharp, over-protective voice.

'We can't all go in there at once. It'll frighten her and we need her on our side if we're to find out who her father really is. Trust me, honey, when I say I know she'll not harm me. I know this woman. Her heart and soul are good and I need to gain her trust if we're to succeed.'

'OK, we'll give you thirty minutes, but Jack and I are coming with you to the apartment. We'll stay hidden so she won't see us but I need to be close to you just in case. That's the way it's going to be. I don't want you to be another sacrificial victim. Robyn and Sam can stay in the limousine and keep an eye out in case we have any unexpected visitors,' Monty growls.

With that the three of us make our way towards the apartment, while Robyn and Sam make themselves comfortable in the limousine. With Jack and Monty hiding in the corridor I knock on the door, contemplating how far we've managed to come in our quest for the truth on behalf of our American spirit. At last I will be face to face with his killer, yet at the same time I feel protective towards her.

Suddenly she's standing before me; the most beautiful vision I've ever seen, with long golden hair tumbling around her luminous face with its flawless complexion and magnetic blue eyes that draw you into her completely. I see the most divine, shimmering light emitting from her, which glows brighter and brighter. She has a gentleness about her that leaves you feeling completely fulfilled. She's an enchantress. She's the embodiment of good. I know this woman. I've seen her many times before in my visions. She's the bringer of unconditional and all-encompassing love; a guardian angel. Yet I sense she is of flesh and blood and not of the spirit world, but somehow there's something about her, which transcends all mortal creatures.

She's not a murderer. She doesn't destroy. She gives life. I know even before she speaks that she's Mallon's saviour and his only hope for redemption. But should she fail then brightness becomes darkness. I immediately feel a whirlwind of emotions. Euphoria at finding her but complete and utter abhorrence should I fail in my quest, and she, along with her father, is damned forever to the 'dark life'.

'Come in, Charity, I've been expecting you.'

Within seconds of hearing her voice and being in her presence I know she is an innocent, an 'attendant spirit', one of God's divine messengers; reborn into mortal form. A female Godchild.

'If you knew who I was, why wait for me to seek you out? You must know my journey for the truth has been a dangerous and treacherous one. Why have I been chosen and what is it that you want from me? You've the protection of the "Supreme Being". What can I do that you can't?' I ask, my voice trembling and my body shivering with

127

emotion: anger at God and the dark forces he's led me into, but completeness at finally meeting Charlotte.

'Please don't be angry, Charity, I couldn't come to you for the journey for truth is not a simple one. My father must prove himself worthy of redemption and in order for him to be saved the truth can only be told through you. As you uncover each layer of my father's dark secret, the closer he is to the light. I can't tell you his secret, as you must complete your journey in order to save him and me from the "Unholy One". You're protected by God's light. He believes in you. He knows you'll complete your quest. Don't worry, your gift of "clear seeing" and the love and power of the RING will be your strength.'

As I listen I begin to understand; her father took everything and gave nothing and now he must feel the pain and anguish of sacrifice and loss, the dark and light coming together to make him whole. As I seek the answers to my questions I know that only some will be answered, as my journey is not over yet.

'Why kill your father in such a barbarous way? Everything I sense about you tells me you're not the messenger of death but the giver of life. Who is your mother and where is she? Who is the boy in my vision by the stream and who are the other family? Who are Alex and Lucy really and why did they kill Donald Coleman? Has Nancy signed a contract with the Enchanter? Who was your father before he became Stephen Mallon and whose soul did he steal? Why does God offer him the light of redemption and not others?' Then, suddenly, without hesitation I ask the question I've hidden deep within me since childhood, fearful that the answer will be my undoing. 'Who is my father and where is he?'

As she listens, with a calmness about her, I see a beautiful golden aura around her, which begins to float towards me, encompassing my whole body, and I feel lifted into another dimension. A place where my mind, body and soul melt into one and I feel at peace. For the first time I'm not afraid of the answer. Then she lays her hand on my forehead with its heat penetrating my mind and thoughts as she says gently 'Close your eyes, Charity, and see.'

Suddenly I'm in another world, beyond the laws of nature, a supernatural world full of forces and beings unlike any I've seen or encountered before. I see angels, a beautiful world of healing angels. There are archangels in full armour wielding their swords, and guardian angels full of love, the angels of dreams and angels of forgiveness, ideas and inspiration. Angels of miracles, music and new beginnings and more all surrounded by the most glorious light. And all of them bringing the message of the 'One True Being'. I see the world of God. I see the afterlife. I see Heaven. Then it appears: a unicorn, with flowing white tail and mane, with a beautiful long white horn growing from its forehead. It flies amongst the angels with magnificent white wings as it bewitches and beguiles all that it comes into contact with. It's the embodiment of enchantment. Then suddenly there's a dark cloud over my beautiful vision, and enchantment again has proved to be a false illusion. The dark forces have penetrated this glorious vision and the demons enter. The unicorn begins to change with its magnificent horn metamorphosing into a black two-headed serpent with long red tongues and pointed yellow teeth. Within seconds the unicorn is no more and the demon serpent slithers amongst the angels hissing and spitting its poisonous venom as it seeks out its prey. Suddenly it stops and rises up until it's face to face with two archangels, who are magnificent in their splendour, with golden armour, wings of blue and golden feathers cascading down their backs and wielding swords in their right hands. They stand astride, guarding a golden throne, which emits the brightest of lights. On the throne is the most powerful angel of all, the 'One True Being'. He floats on his throne amongst a brilliant golden, flameless light. His wings spread upwards, rising high behind him, glowing with the flames of life, with feathers magnificent in their colours ranging from brilliant white in the centre fusing into blues and greens, finally accumulating into one golden light that eclipses all others. His face is indescribable in its beauty and wisdom. If this is God and the afterlife then death holds no fear for me.

I watch the two-headed serpent moving in a winding course, slithering and sliding towards the archangels who remain still wielding their swords of justice. It tries to tempt them with dark and evil thoughts, hissing and whispering as it slithers over their bodies, but they remain strong, glowing in the light of God. Slowly the serpent begins to shrivel, loosing its powers as it's unable to draw them into the dark world of demons. Then suddenly it lashes out and sinks its teeth into the neck of one of the archangels, who with one sweeping stroke of his mighty sword, detaches its head from its body, throwing it back into the darkness. Slowly the vision begins to disappear and I'm back with Charlotte trying to unravel its meaning.

'I don't understand the vision? What has it to do with your father, and where is *my* father in this vision? Surely you can answer these questions? Help me to help your father, Charlotte. Help me to understand who my father was,' I ask, feeling bewildered and confused, for in seeking the truth for Charlotte's father my own father's fate has crossed my path and opened my heart and mind to thoughts I'd kept hidden. Now my thirst for knowledge will not cease until I know the truth, whatever the consequences or price.

'I can tell you only this. The unicorn was a serpent sent by the Anti-Angel, whom we know as the "Lord of Darkness", the Devil, who was once one of God's greatest archangels; Lucifer, who was banished forever when he went over to the dark side, and whose sole existence is to tempt all that is good into his world of darkness and demons. The serpent couldn't tempt God's great protectors, his magnificent archangels Michael and Sovereign, so bit Archangel Michael, using its poisonous venom to slowly seep through his mind and thoughts until eventually he fell from grace. To discover the fate of Archangel Michael and your father you must continue on your quest and in doing so will uncover the dark secret of my father and unlock the key to his redemption.'

As I listen to Charlotte I begin to realise that I've been chosen for a reason. I know now that both Stephen Mallon and my father are bound together in some way. Their paths have crossed and in doing so are intrinsically linked to mine. When I unlock the key to Mallon's past I also open the door to my father's and in turn discover the missing pieces of myself. Now, more than ever, it's imperative that I complete my quest to save Mallon's soul, which in so doing, I now believe will also save my father's. Anxiously I ask Charlotte, 'Once again I beseech you. What's the meaning behind the ritual of your father's death and the sign of the cross cut into his body? Why desiccate his body of all its blood, and who is your mother?' Just as I was about to continue Charlotte interrupts.

'Stop, Charity: I can answer only some of your questions. For the others you must look for the "Angel of Signs" who will show you the way to the truth. I was born to save my father. My mother was the "Angel of Forgiveness" sent by God in mortal form to seduce him. I bring the power of inception. I was born into a mortal body but my soul and spirit is that of the angels. I'm the "Angel of New Beginnings". I see things that no mortal can. I have the gift of "clear seeing" and the power of the angels within me. I, like you, have the power to communicate between the mortal and spirit world. I'm an inceptor of the highest level and I know what my future holds and it's in your hands. You've been chosen because part of you is part of me. Your great gift has been passed to you for a reason. When you reach the end of your quest all will become clear and you'll finally feel complete.'

Then she stops for a moment and smiles; a smile I recognise, for it's the same smile I have when I think of Ma. Then she continues. 'My mother stayed with me until I was eighteen years old, then returned to the world of angels. My father loved her deeply for she brought him forgiveness and I bring him genesis. He's not dead. His body is without blood, lying in a state of catalepsy, waiting for redemption. Remember your vision, Charity, and the truth will be yours. Now you must continue on your quest.'

As I listen I sense her time here in the mortal world will soon be over and that her destiny, along with her father's, lies in my hands. I'm afraid for her, for I fear she is waiting for Armageddon.

Gently, I say, 'Be careful, Charlotte, the Dark Trio will find you soon.'

She takes my hand and holds it tightly saying, 'Don't worry, I'm expecting them. We'll meet again, my dear Charity, at the final reckoning.'

I leave, knowing that the next time we meet it will be for the last time.

'Well, what did she say? What's she like? Did she kill her father?' asks Sam, all animated as we return to the

132

limousine. Robyn waits patiently for me to reply, sensing that I'm afraid.

I sit for a few moments in silence as Sam's voice drifts over me into a distant sound. My world seems to be turning inward and all that I knew and felt sure about now seems to be evaporating. I was always so sure of who I was and my destiny as an inceptor. Now I feel there's a part of me that has been kept in the darkness, waiting to emerge; the part that belongs to my father.

'Are you all right, spud, you seem so distant? She didn't harm you in anyway?' Monty asks, looking bewildered and a little afraid as he holds my hand tightly, while Jack drives us to the airport. Still unable to mention my father, I reply, 'She showed me a vision full of angels. I'm not sure what it means yet, but when we get to Church Town and find David Shield then I'll understand.'

11

Angel of Signs

As we drive into Church Town it epitomises everything
you imagine a small sleepy Southern American town to
be. With its large welcome sign, picturesque white houses
with their porches and picket fences in long leafy lanes
leading to the town centre, encircled by more white
buildings. The local town hall and church with steeple
and homely-looking shops, all give that quintessential
illusion of Shangri-La. We park outside the church and
feel the glare of everyone in town upon us.

'I don't think they get many visitors, especially ones
like us by the looks of it. There's something creepy about
this town, it's almost too perfect, like it doesn't really
exist except in our imagination,' Robyn says warily, as
we make our way along the path to the church.

'I know what you mean. It appears all cosy and welcoming,
but like a spider, it's enticing you into its web only to be
eaten,' replies Sam, as we enter the church looking for
the local priest in the hope that he can point us in the
direction of David Shield.

We're greeted by a tall, skinny man aged about 55,
dressed in a black priestly gown and white collar with
thick, almost white, hair, a pale, ghoulish face with hollow
dark eyes and a cold, detached smile. Creepily he says in
a bleak Southern accent, 'Welcome to the house of God

134

and how can I be of assistance to you good people.'

'We're looking for David Shield, who I understand used to be the vicar of the church several years ago,' I reply, sensing that somehow he was expecting us and not surprised at my question as he smiles coldly, rubbing his hands continuously, indicating that perhaps he's more afraid of us than we are of him, yet giving the illusion of friendship.

'Ah, poor David, such a brilliant priest in his time, but now sadly a mere shadow of the man he once was. What is it that brings you all the way here to see him? I've known David for years and don't recall him ever mentioning knowing anybody from England? Is it something that I can help you with?'

'That's kind of you but it's David we need to speak to and would really appreciate your help,' replies Monty as he moves closer towards him in a subtle, slightly menacing manner that indicates it would be advisable for him to help us. Sometimes when the situation requires it Monty can do threatening very well.

He turns away from Monty and looks straight into my eyes, almost as if he were playing a game, taunting me, knowing that whatever he's about to impart will be of no consequence as we'll be powerless.

'Everyone knows David. He lives in an old house in the woods about seven miles outside town. Follow the sign leading to Homerville and you'll see a dirt track leading off the road, which will take you to David, but be careful for the road to Homerville can be a treacherous one,' he says insincerely, while smiling away in that creepy, cold manner of his. For a second my gift allows me to see his real persona, a dark, shadowy ghost-like figure. This is no priest, I think to myself, but another disciple of the Devil. Quickly we leave, feeling relieved to be out in the fresh air as the house of God didn't feel particularly warm or welcoming.

'What's our next move then? Straight to the woods or check out the Mallon Estate first?' Robyn asks as we make our way back to the car.

'The sooner we leave this town the safer we'll be. Visiting the "den of darkness" is not advisable. Let's see what this David Shield can tell us first. Anyway it's on the road to Homerville, which is where we're heading,' I reply, anxious to put distance between the dark forces, lurking under the idyllic illusion of Church Town, and us.

We all agree, as Jack drives off, following the sign leading to Homerville, but there's an unspoken uneasiness between us, with the last words of our ghoulish priest echoing in our minds. 'Be careful, for the road to Homerville can be a treacherous one.'

As we drive along, the day begins to change from brightness to darkness and there's an eerie wind following us, which moves over the car, bringing a dark shadow that eclipses our vision. We turn off the main road onto the dirt track, following the arrow that says 'The Old Lodge'. The wind becomes stronger, almost taking the car off the road as Jack tries to avoid flying branches, leaves, stones and even old tree trunks. There's a voice within the wind that seems to be whispering to us, telling us, 'The truth is darkness'. It repeats it over and over again, seeping into our thoughts, trying to destroy our strength, but no words are needed between us as we hold strong in our belief in each other and the real truth.

Finally we arrive at our destination and see before us a broken, pitiful remnant of a once grand and noble house – The Old Lodge, set deep within the woods, surrounded by tall oppressive trees that eclipse all light, emitting whispers of pain and loss. A great sadness comes over us as we make our way to the door, for this is not a happy place. It screams of anguish and despair where only the broken and damned remain and where the light of happiness and hope has been extinguished. As I knock on the door my heart bleeds for the 'great loss' of the man who's about to let us into his world.

The door opens and there he stands, a tragic wreck of a man aged about 45 with his looks now ravaged by the despair of hopelessness, but as I look deeper I see a once proud man full of life. His whole aura is that of a man beaten down and ground into the dirt, his face drawn and pale with deep lines of sorrow etched across it. He stands stooped with his body almost emaciated and crumbling with the lack of hope and love; the two things I sense were his 'food of life'. I begin to speak but before I can utter a single word he says in a broken, defeated voice, 'So you've finally arrived – then you'd better come in.'

He leads us into a large, bleak hallway that's littered with paintings all over the walls and floors, depicting dark, shadowy figures of abandonment and loss. We climb over them like an obstacle course, finally reaching what appears to be the lounge, which has more paintings, all crying with the utter despair and loss of the man who created them. He indicates for us to sit down while slumping into a large threadbare chair in front of a huge crumbling open fireplace, above which sits a portrait that's torn and worn with age. As I look closer there's no mistaking the handsome man in it who stands proud in his priestly gown, glowing with hope and love. Indeed, as I look at the man slumped in the chair, comparing him to the one in the portrait, an overwhelming feeling of admiration and pity races through me. Admiration for the man he once was and pity for the man he's become and the price he's paid for remaining true to his God.

Surely such a man deserves not to be abandoned but cherished and rewarded?

Wearily, he continues. 'You're too late, I've been waiting for years. Praying to a God that's forsaken me to come and destroy the Lord of Darkness. Now his children will soon be all powerful and our world will become theirs and we'll all be damned for ever.'

As he speaks, the tears trickle down his face while he stares blankly into the fire, then briefly glances at the portrait above, wistful for the man that he once was. I move towards him and kneel down, cupping his hands in mine, gently saying, while looking deep into his eyes, 'Your God hasn't forsaken you and your prayers have been answered. The journey has been a long and treacherous one but the end is coming. Don't falter now. Be strong and believe. Join with us and feel the power of the "One True Being" and know God's love and protection once more.'

I stand, pulling him close to me until we are both directly beneath his portrait and continue. 'David Shield, I beseech you to join us in our quest for truth and redemption where the final reckoning will be ours.'

He stares straight through me, then turns and looks at his portrait, only this time a smile crosses his lips and a light returns to his eyes, and I know he's back. Then without hesitation he asks, 'What do you want from me? Ask and I shall give, for I've fought so hard and waited so long. Whatever I've left in me is now yours.'

We sit again, only this time the room feels different. Gone is the feeling of anguish and despair, replaced by hope and light. Gently, I tell him our story so far and the journey we've made to reach him, culminating by asking, 'Do you know who the real Stephen Mallon is?'

He smiles, while placing another log on the fire and then begins to tell his story.

* * *

'I first met Stephen twenty-five years ago when he arrived in Church Town from Homerville. He was extremely handsome, beguiling all around him, and soon the town was his, but I saw beyond the illusion of enchantment into his soul and saw darkness. From that moment until now I battled against the evil that was within him only to be driven from my own church and almost into the pit of madness. I went to Homerville in search of the truth and found a town where only the dead live. That's what he did. He came bearing gifts and then sucked the life from you leaving only despair and blackness behind. Soon Church Town will become another Homerville, only now its masters will be Alex and Lucy, the "children of darkness". Once they become all powerful they'll spore their "seed of evil" throughout the earth until there's no more goodness left. Soon it will be the first of June and then the darkness will descend upon us and we shall be damned for all eternity.'

His hands begin to shake and an impending sense of doom overtakes him, almost sucking the life from him. Quickly Monty says, 'There's still time, tell us what you know and together we'll beat this evil.' He looks up at Monty and feels his strength, then continues.

'I discovered there were two souls within him. One stolen from a young boy aged about fifteen whose name was Shane Colby. He was a happy, innocent boy who loved the outdoors and playing in a stream not far from where he lived. One day, forty-five years ago he went out to play, never to return. He had two brothers named Abraham and Kane who are still alive today, living in the same house. But to this day they don't know what happened to their brother. Yet each month for the last forty years they've received an anonymous allowance. They

139

have no idea who sends it or why, but somehow know it's connected to their lost brother. Why and how Shane Colby's soul was taken I've never been able to discover, but I know he was one of the souls trapped inside Stephen. Perhaps you're the ones sent to find the truth behind Shane Colby. To find the brothers you must go past Homerville until you reach a small town called Summer Town. Just outside, near a place called Crystal Stream you'll find the brothers.'

My heart begins to beat faster and I feel my throat drying with panic for somehow I fear that the other soul has something to do with my father. I ask the question that I don't want answered, knowing that my destiny is to seek the truth no matter what the consequences. 'What about the other soul? Who does it belong to?'

He looks at me and I see he knows. His eyes show pity and sadness and for a moment I'm afraid. I wasn't even born when my father 'left', yet his destiny has become mine. Can I have evil within me? My mother's last words ring loud in my head. 'He gave himself over to the dark side and is no longer.' Then he continues.

'There were stories of a young boy called Michael, travelling through the South, doing all manner of jobs, who had no last name and no one knew where he came from. He was a handsome boy who grew into a strong and wilful man yet there was a goodness about him that transcended all others. Then on the first of June forty years ago, aged twenty, in the town of Homerville, he disappeared, never to be seen again. Suddenly on the same day another handsome man appeared of similar age and looks with no past, but whose soul was dark. Then the legend begins. From lost boy to wandering boy to wilful young man to handsome, evil man; one soul passes to another by taking another; boy to boy and man to man to beget Stephen Mallon. How and why and who, I

140

can't answer, but I do know this: Alex and Lucy Mallon were born evil – their souls belong to them. They're the children of darkness, each born on the first of June at ten-thirty in the morning. Everything leads to that date. The world we know will change for ever on that date and we're powerless to stop it.'

As we listen, I see it clearly. Everything is leading us to Crystal Stream where it all began and where I'll find the truth, not only for Mallon, but also my father. I look into the eyes of David Shield and see his fear, yet know there's still faith and strength deep within him just waiting to be ignited. I lean over towards him and ask, 'Come with us to Crystal Stream and finish your battle with evil. Only then will you feel at peace and know God again.'

He sits for what seems an eternity, staring into the abyss and then replies, 'I'm done with fighting. For years I've been waiting for God to give me a sign and now I know he has. It's only now that I understand. He never left me. My task was to know my enemy. Your journey has led you to me so that I can pass this knowledge on to you. My years haven't been wasted and now I can rest in peace. God be with you on your quest. You don't need me. My job is done.'

We say goodbye, leaving behind a man upright and strong, with hope and pride in his eyes; not the defeated wretch that first greeted us. As we make our way back to the car the wind still howls and the trees still whisper, but the message is different. There's a light glimmering through the trees, shining down on The Old Lodge; it's the light of hope, which has been ignited back into the soul of David Shield.

Soon we're on the road again; next stop Homerville, the

141

birthplace of Mallon. As we drive along my mind begins to wander into the darkest corners of my fears. I'm coming closer to the end of my quest and to finding the truth behind our American spirit and his redemption, but what of my father? Will there be redemption for him? Or will the dark spirits of the past be calling upon me to collect his debt (my soul), leaving me at the mercy of the evil spirits of darkness? I feel Monty's hand upon mine and hear his soft words.

'I know there's something you're not telling me, spud; we've never had secrets from each other, please don't shut me out. Tell me what's troubling you and we'll fight it together.'

I look around and see my beloved Monty and the rest of the RING and know he's right. I must bring them into my world and feel the strength of their love and protection. Slowly I tell them of my vision with Charlotte and her message and for the first time I mention my father and the fear of retribution being called upon his daughter for his past sins. Tears trickle down my face and for a moment all my inner powers and strength seem to leave me and for the first time I experience the dark pit of hopelessness. The thought that I may have a dark soul inside waiting to be awakened paralyses me with fear. Then I hear Monty's words.

'You're the strongest and noblest person I've ever known, with the truest of souls, which no dark force can enter or destroy. Together we'll face these evil spirits of the dark and WIN.'

'Remember who you are and your powerful gift and that you're being guided and protected by the angels of light and that truth and redemption will be ours,' says Robyn with a force and strength I've never heard before, which together with Sam and Jack's words of love and strength pull me back from the shadowy world of despair.

                              *   *   *

We continue on our journey towards Homerville and as
we draw closer a strange melancholy begins to descend
upon us. Then from within the mist we see the town
looming before us, but unlike Church Town it doesn't
have the illusion of safety and warmth. There are no
pretty white houses in leafy lanes with a welcoming town
centre. Instead, dark Gothic buildings with pointed arches
and ugly ghoulish figures astride their bleak porches greet
us. Even though it's nearing the end of May there are
dead leaves, black clouds and a bitter wind that eclipses
the whole town.

We make our way to the local sheriff's office and park
outside. Unlike Church Town we're not entering Shangri-
La, but a dark underworld where evil pours from every
orifice; a dead town where only the dead live. I can smell
it as I feel my throat choking on its oppressive air, almost
sucking the life from me. As we enter the sheriff's office
and make our way to the front desk all eyes are upon
us, burning their way into our thoughts.

Immediately I sense a great danger and begin to look
more deeply at the people in the room. As I look around
my gift of 'clear seeing' shows me their true faces.
Outwardly they look like us but underneath they're wild
predatory canine mammals: wolf people. Evil wolf spirits
who eat ravenously on human souls until there's no
goodness left except the outer shell, which hides the
hideous animal within. They come from the 'dark life'
with the Devil as their master. They feed on mortals
until they own their souls and then live on in their shell-
like bodies to spread their evil. One bite at the stroke of
midnight opens the door into your mind, spreading their
dark thoughts slowly through your body. Seven days must
pass, then on the stroke of midnight the second bite

seals your fate forever. Before the seventh day has passed if the wolf spirit that has taken first blood is destroyed your soul is returned to you, but only a bullet from one that is pure in thought can kill a wolf spirit. Nothing can save you once the second bite has been taken.

My blood runs cold with the thought that we're standing in a room full of wolf spirits, whose sole existence is to taste the warm blood of mortals. I see them licking their lips with the slow trickle of saliva dripping from their sharp yellow teeth in hungry anticipation of their next victims. Fortunately for us the day is still light and midnight is seven hours away. I whisper to Robyn to use her gift to look beyond the human illusion, for although it's still in its infancy I know if she concentrates she will see. The look of pure fear on her face says it all. Within seconds Monty, Jack and Sam also feel the evil presence and realise that the quicker we get out of town the safer we'll be.

A podgy, pale-faced man, aged about 35 with wiry black hair and a rough, spiteful manner, greets us. He grins, showing a mouthful of stained, uneven teeth and a bad case of halitosis, which makes close contact a non-starter.

'My name is Charity Holmes and I'd like to speak to the sheriff,' I say, knowing that he's already expecting us. For the closer we get to Summer Town and Crystal Stream the more dangerous our journey becomes.

'The sheriff's a very busy man. What do you want to see him about?' he asks with a gruff, unpleasant voice as his breath floats in the air, almost knocking us out with its pungent smell of death and disease. My gift of 'clear seeing' enables me to see his two heads as he constantly metamorphoses from mortal to wolf spirit. Sergeant Dredge is a prince in comparison.

'Just say I'm a friend of Stephen Mallon. I'm sure he'll want see to me then,' I reply, smiling sweetly while covering my mouth and nose with my hand as the stench of death becomes unbearable. He makes a quick phone call then leads us past all the lip-smacking wolf spirits into a large office surrounded by numerous wolf heads mounted on the walls. Seated at a large desk in the middle of the room is the most obnoxious, ugly-looking man I've ever set eyes upon. As we're shown to our chairs we're all *simpatico* in our feelings of disdain for the creature that sits before us – an incredibly fat man, who can barely fit into the chair with a huge barbarous head and no neck. His cheeks are so fat and bloated that he can hardly speak without stopping to draw a breath every few seconds. The podgy man on the desk appears positively handsome in comparison. As he greets us with a breathless, arrogant voice, his halitosis almost knocks us off our chairs. Robyn and I look at each other, for we can see the other head, which is even uglier. An enormous black wolf head with piercing yellow eyes, sharp pointed nose and ears, long stained teeth with sabre-like edges. There's no doubting that this wolf spirit has gorged himself on many a mortal soul, his greed endless in its need for the taste of human blood. Once again it's apparent to us all that a short visit and even shorter conversation with this chap is advisable.

'So you're a friend of Stephen? Strange, I've never heard him speak of you before. Stephen wasn't a man who had "friends",' he says, catching his breath, almost unable to speak with the discomfort of such a bloated head, which I'm half expecting to explode at any moment.

'I'm on a quest on behalf of my client Stephen Mallon, who in death has passed on to me his wishes for truth and redemption. My quest has led my colleagues and I to Homerville where I believe forty years ago he killed a man, but was never convicted? I understand you were the local deputy at the time investigating the murder.

145

Can you enlighten us as to what really happened and how he was involved?'

He stares directly at me, smirking. I try to remain calm as my gift of 'clear seeing' shows me his true self, the ugly wolf spirit. Then he answers coldly, 'Truth and redemption – neither are going to be Stephen's. He collected while alive and now he's dead he must pay what is due. Soon he'll be with our Master and at his mercy. You'll not be able to save him now.'

He doesn't seem surprised by my question or our presence. In fact he appears somewhat bemused that Mallon was seeking redemption and that we have made it this far. I sense that he feels our time is running out and it doesn't matter to him what he tells us as it will be too late. He continues.

'There was a fire in which the local money lender died and Stephen was a suspect at the time, but nothing was ever proven against him. Eventually he took over the business and his career continued to flourish. It's a small town and people here fall into two categories, the takers and the losers. Stephen was a taker. Those who survive in Homerville are takers. The losers; well there isn't much left of them,' he says, grinning and licking his lips while the other two deputies in the room seem to be anticipating their next meal. I decide that we need to speed things up and get out of Homerville fast.

'I sense that whenever Stephen "took" you were also collecting. The Master will be collecting your dues soon and somehow I don't think you'll have anybody seeking redemption for your soul. An eternity in the "dark life" as a "loser" will be your punishment so perhaps it wouldn't do you any harm to gain a few credits; just in case your Master loses this battle.'

The thought of being a 'loser' for all eternity seems to wipe the grin off his face and for the first time his own

146

destiny becomes an issue. I can see his ugly wolf brain contemplating the terrifying thought of what his dark future holds and he doesn't like it. He was once a man. Wolf spirits only come about through pure lust and greed. Once your soul gives over to the dark side of your nature and you only live to 'take', that's when the Devil strikes and you become his. Somewhere within this ugly creature there still remains a piece of the man. If I can awaken the fears of the man then perhaps he will see his destiny, even if only for a few seconds, and know that maybe one good deed may redeem him later. Then somewhat more thoughtfully and less arrogantly, he says, 'Stephen has the hand of God on him, that's all I can tell you.'

Suddenly my heart skips a beat and for the first time I feel we're nearing the end of our quest. Then Monty asks, 'What do you mean the "hand of God"?'

I see the sheriff struggling with the two souls within him. The man is weak and the wolf spirit strong, but the fear of suddenly realising that his fate is similar to Mallon's is stronger at this moment in time and so he replies, 'Stephen was led into the dark by a trick. He comes from a much higher place than you or I. I can tell you no more or my fate will be sealed before midnight tonight; you must go to Summer Town and Crystal Stream to find the answer. But be careful, for your journey there will take you into the midnight hour and the woods are full of creatures of the night waiting for lost travellers.'

On those last words we leave without looking back, relieved to put distance between us and the wolf spirits, but wary of what lies ahead as darkness descends and our journey will cross the midnight hour before we reach Summer Town. As Jack drives along we chat about events so far, partly to check our facts and partly to distract us from the sounds of the night. Robyn picks up on the sheriff's last words.

'What do you think he meant by "led into the dark by a trick", and he comes from a "higher" place than us?'

Sam ponders for a moment then chips in with her thoughts. 'Perhaps he meant that the soul stolen by Mallon belonged to someone who was once a priest or something like that. I mean, that's the ultimate feeling of satisfaction for evil to corrupt pure goodness.'

Monty and Jack put in their two pennies' worth by commenting that perhaps the stolen soul was from someone yet untouched by human weakness, a newborn child or very young boy like the boy in my vision. I think back to the vision shown to me by Charlotte Mallon, where the unicorn entered the world of healing angels only to turn into a serpent sent by the Devil to corrupt the angels of light.

'The vision shown to me by Charlotte Mallon is the key. I believe Mallon is connected to the afterlife and has been given a chance by God, through us, to return there. Our journey ends at Crystal Stream where it all began forty-five years ago,' I say, while quietly thinking that somewhere in our quest lays not only the truth behind the dark secret of Mallon, but also that of my father's fate. We continue on our journey as the night begins to draw in and after stopping *en route* at a small roadside café we set off again. Monty takes over the driving, while Jack and the rest of us sleep, ready to gather our strength for what lies ahead. Suddenly we're awoken by Monty braking sharply, causing the car to swerve off the road, almost turning on its side and finally stopping at the edge of the woods.

'What happened?' shouts Jack as we all pull ourselves together.

'I thought I saw something in the middle of the road. They looked like huge demonic yellow eyes staring straight at me from the darkness. They just appeared from nowhere and startled me,' replies Monty, looking a little shaken but unhurt.

Then we hear it: a terrifying howl that pierces our ears, almost bursting our eardrums. It starts to get louder and louder as suddenly it appears from the darkness of the woods, moving towards us. The biggest, darkest, most hideous wolf spirit I've ever seen, with a massive black head and snarling pointed sabre teeth dripping with saliva. Its terrifying howls echo through the night, while it races towards us ready to tear its victims to pieces. I look at my watch and see the time is one minute past midnight.

'Oh God, oh God, we're done for,' shouts Sam as Monty tries to start the car and Jack fires his gun helplessly into the dark trying to kill the beast. Nothing will kill a wolf spirit when it's drawing first blood at the midnight hour except one that's pure in thought and there's no mortal that fits that description. Unless within the next few seconds divine intervention is to be our saviour, we're lost. Then as we stand helplessly awaiting our fate and the wolf spirit is almost upon us another beast suddenly appears from within the darkness. It's another wolf spirit, whose coat is pure white and glows in the dark. It has jet-black eyes and snarling teeth. The black wolf spirit turns and the two face each other, baring their teeth, snarling and howling with saliva dripping from their mouths, their eyes flashing in the dark as they leap at each other, sinking their teeth deep into each other's throats. They tear away pieces of flesh, drawing blood while flying through the air. They howl and cry as the two rip each other apart until finally the white wolf spirit sinks his teeth deep into the throat of the black one until he cries the last howl of death.

The five of us stand riveted in shock, looking at the half-dead wolf spirit standing before us. His white coat is drenched with blood, dripping from the tear marks in his throat as he stands triumphantly over his kill. Suddenly he moves, limping towards us until he stands directly before me, staring straight into my eyes. I look deep into his black eyes until I see a white light, which shows the vision of a man. A tall handsome man wearing a long black cloak, who looks back at me and smiles. I feel an instant connection with this man and know immediately who he is: my father. Suddenly the vision is gone. The wolf spirit then turns and slowly disappears into the woods.

Monty rushes towards me, almost crushing me in his arms, his body trembling with fear, saying, 'Are you OK, spud?'

Robyn takes my hand, gently saying, 'He looked at you as if he knew you and came to protect you. What face did you see behind the wolf spirit?'

Sam and Jack look on shaken while I try to answer.

'I saw a man smiling at me and I think that man was my father. He was wearing the coat of the "dark life", the same coat that Mallon wore in his materialisation; the "cloak of death". Alex Mallon said my father was waiting for me when I had my "flashing vision" back at the Davenport Mansion and Ma told me before she died that my father "gave himself over to the dark side". Charlotte Mallon showed me in her vision of the healing angels that both Mallon and my father's paths have crossed, which is intrinsically linked to mine. I now believe my destiny was already decided before I was born. I know now that my father came to save us in the body of the wolf spirit yet he's trapped in the "dark life". When we find the truth and redeem Mallon my father will also be saved. We must reach Crystal Stream before it's too late.'

We all look at each other in silence for a few moments,

suddenly realising how little control we really have over our own destinies. Monty and Jack sort out the car while Sam, Robyn and I keep our eyes fixed on the dead wolf spirit; just in case. Then we continue our journey on the road to Summer Town and Crystal Stream. The dawn is breaking and we drive into Summer Town, a sleepy, peaceful little place with no town centre, just a few weather-beaten houses, a local grocery store and a garage. It's a poor looking town but exudes a warmth and carefree happiness that envelops you completely. There's no feeling of fear or dread in this town. We park outside the garage and ask an ancient, slow-moving man where we can find Abraham and Kane Colby. An eternity seems to pass before he replies in an almost painfully slow Southern American drawl, 'Abraham and Kane never have visitors. No one here ever has any visitors. Must be something really special to bring visitors all the way out here.'

Then there's a long pause where he seems to forget what the question was, so Jack, impatient as ever, asks again, 'Abraham and Kane Colby. You were about to inform us where we could find them.'

Slowly he replies. 'Abraham and Kane never have visitors. Must be important. Everybody knows where Abraham and Kane live, five miles out near Crystal Stream. Can't miss their rickety old shack – follow the sun and you'll find them.'

Monty fills the car up with petrol and drives towards the sun and Crystal Stream. As we drive along the sun glistens in the distance and a beautiful rainbow marks the way to an old crumbling wooden house deep within the backwoods. We come upon a twisted road running parallel to a lake leading to the house, which has a beautiful waterfall in the backdrop, cascading into the lake. Although

151

the wooden house has seen better days there's a warm, almost magical mist around it, which emits a tranquil feeling of euphoria all around us. Before Monty stops the engine two men appear from the house smiling. Immediately I know they're expecting us and within minutes we find ourselves sitting at a large wooden table in a cramped but cosy little kitchen.

They are two little men in their fifties, almost identical in looks, no more than 5ft 4 inches tall with rosy cheeks, balding heads and pot bellies, dressed in identical check shirts and worn denim overalls. They talk excitedly, finishing each other's sentences as they fuss around, preparing food and drink. As I look around I notice the table is already set for seven places. Before the others or I can utter a word they say excitedly, 'Welcome, welcome. The "Angel of Signs" said you'd come. We've been waiting for forty years and at last you're here. Please eat. What's ours is yours – whatever you need just ask.'

As we tuck into the food I look at the two little men in front of us and see a beautiful golden aura around them. A wonderful feeling of completeness comes over me and I know our journey has reached its end. I look at Robyn and see her smiling and know that she sees and feels it too. At last we'll know the truth about Mallon along with my father's fate and my own destiny. Monty squeezes my hand, as he looks at me lovingly, fearful of what that destiny might be while I say, 'My name is Charity Holmes, and a man named Stephen Mallon, who I believe to be your brother Shane, has charged me with an effort to save his soul from eternal damnation. I accepted his charge and our quest has led us to you. I now charge you to help us complete our quest on behalf of your brother.'

They smile simultaneously, then begin to tell their story.

'Forty-five years ago on the first of June Shane went

152

out to play by the stream, as he had done every day since the age of seven, only this time he never returned. He was fifteen years old and a happy, innocent boy who loved the outdoors and water. We were much younger – aged seven and eleven years and loved each other dearly, so when he didn't return, my father, together with the town's people, searched the stream for his body, but it was never found. Our father searched that stream every day for the next four years but found nothing. It broke his heart and he died shortly before the end of the fourth year. Our mother never recovered from the day Shane disappeared and died within six months of our father's death. We struggled to survive on our own, but then one day, forty years ago, in the fifth year, on the same date Shane disappeared, a miraculous vision appeared before us.

'It was ten-thirty in the morning and we were out by the stream fishing when a brilliant blue light appeared in the sky, which floated towards us until we saw her. An angel. She had the most beautiful face, long golden hair and magnificent gold and blue wings raised high behind her as she floated before us in a shimmering blue robe. She pointed towards us and stardust floated from her fingers down onto our eyes, showing us a vision: It was our brother. We saw him playing by the stream, when a magnificent winged wraith appeared from the sky wielding a sword. Shane looked up at the wraith who cut through him with his sword and instantly the sky was aflame with a blinding light. As the light disappeared Shane and the wraith were gone.'

'What's a wraith?' asks Sam as we all sit riveted, listening to their story.

'It's an apparition of a ghost-like figure seen shortly before death. In this case the wraith was the Archangel Michael before he killed Shane and took his body as his own,' I reply, as I begin to understand why Stephen Mallon, alias Shane Colby, has been given a chance of redemption; the innocent boy and God's greatest Archangel Michael destroyed by the power of the Devil.

'What happened next?' asks Jack, who by now is completely enthralled by their tale.

'The angel then spoke. She said her name was Majesta, the Angel of Signs sent to give us a sign of where Shane is. She told us we must wait, and a woman will come bringing with her truth and redemption. When she comes Shane will be free to join our mother and father in the afterlife. She said there was a man whose soul hangs in the balance of darkness waiting to be released and this man's soul is joined together with Shane's. When his soul is released then so will Shane's and we will at last be free from our burden of waiting. She then said we would receive a gift of money each month from a stranger, which we must accept without question, as this gift will help us endure the years of waiting. Then as she floated back into the heavens we asked her, "How will we know this woman?" to which she replied, "Look for the sign of the rainbow and guide her to it." Today the rainbow appeared and then you came.'

With those words they point through the kitchen window towards the stream where the rainbow that guided us to the house now calls us to it. We follow them to the rainbow, which stops by the waterfall, and we feel the magic emanating from it. As we gaze at the splendour of its colours and feel the warmth of its mystical light she appears from within the circle of light, a beautiful blue angel just as the brothers described. She floats towards us with her magnificent feathered wings spread high above her, encased in a golden light, which glistens on her long flowing hair. As she draws closer she stretches out her arms until her fingertips almost touch my face.

154

The golden light moves down her arms until I feel its warmth upon my face and I hear her voice.

'See the sign of truth, Charity, and know what you must do.'

Suddenly I see it all. 'Flashing visions' appear before me one after the other and then I understand the words of David Shield. From lost boy to wandering boy to wilful young man to handsome evil man; one soul passes to another by taking another; from boy to boy and man to man to beget Stephen Mallon.

I see the Archangel Michael bitten by a serpent sent by Lucifer the Anti-Angel (the Devil), from the 'dark life', and feel its poison racing through his body, corrupting his mind with the darkest of thoughts. I feel his desires for the warmth of a human body and finally see him descending to earth to take the body of Shane Colby, who must be young and pure of heart. I see Archangel Michael in the body of Shane, wandering through the years experiencing the wonders of being mortal until he reaches Homerville.

Another vision appears of the Enchanter (the Devil) visiting Michael in his dreams, corrupting his mind so he can take his soul, fulfilling his dream of the ultimate prize: to possess the soul of God's greatest and most powerful archangel. But first he must steal another soul to give life to Stephen Mallon. Then I see the vision that tells my destiny. I see a young handsome man somewhere in England, sitting at a bar in a hotel, drinking and laughing. He's celebrating with friends. He's going to be a father; my father. I hear his laughter and feel his joy as he leaves the bar, waving goodbye to his friends, while waiting for a taxi in the rain. As he waits a man approaches, drawing a knife, asking for his money, but my father tries to take the knife and they struggle. Suddenly he's lying in the middle of the road, stabbed four times forming the sign of the cross, as the man disappears into emptiness. I hear his cries of death. Within seconds I see another vision and hear the cries of life and the birth of Stephen Mallon. I see a clock and a date. The time is 10.30 a.m. and the date is 1st June. The loss and pain I feel is unbearable as the tears flow and I see the next vision: empty hollow blackness, an endless pit of despair and hopelessness. Through this blackness I see three distant figures wandering endlessly, unable to find a way out. Three souls trapped in an eternity of darkness, unable to feel the comfort of either the 'middle' or afterlife, waiting for redemption; the souls of Archangel Michael, Shane Colby and my father. Three souls required for the rebirth of one. One soul passes to another by taking another. From boy to boy and man to man to beget Stephen Mallon, the Devil incarnate.

Then I see the final vision: Nancy Coleman making love to Stephen Mallon and the birth of Alex and Lucy, both of whom are born on 1st June at 10.30 a.m. It is the ultimate victory; the children of the Devil born into the mortal world in human bodies, ready to spread their seed throughout the earth once the 'shell of their father' is buried and the contract is sealed, and the three souls trapped in the darkness are condemned to an eternity in the 'dark life' (Hell).

Finally I see the truth behind the dark secret of Stephen Mallon. He's the Devil incarnate. Evil personified. The shell of a human man used to beget the children of the Antichrist, Lucifer. They must not be allowed to live on. They must be destroyed.

We can't allow the body of Stephen Mallon to die on 1st June at 10.30 a.m. or the souls of my father, Shane Colby and the Archangel Michael are lost for all eternity to the evil spirits of the dark and the world as we know it will change forever. Then, suddenly, the light is gone and the Angel of Signs disappears into the rainbow, which slowly descends into the water. I turn to the others and say, 'We must return to England at once. The funeral of Stephen Mallon must not go ahead. We have to stop it. The final reckoning is coming.'

12

The Final Reckoning

As we park ourselves in our favourite chairs by the fireplace and Aunt Lizzy serves up her notoriously tempting toasted sandwiches and tea we all breathe a big sigh of relief at being home.

'It's so good to have you all back, for sure the house was a cold place without yah with its big empty rooms and no one to cook for,' Aunt Lizzy says softly as she joins us by the fire with her own special extra-large mug (for her lips only) of strong tea and an enormous plate of sandwiches. For a while we sit, safely enjoying the warmth and cosiness of the fire and our love for each other, for soon we'll have to face the final reckoning and battle against the Lord of Darkness.

'What a heinous burden Mallon had to endure for forty years. Three souls trapped inside his body, lost in the pit of darkness; Shane Colby, the Archangel Michael and your father, three innocents to beget the darkest demon of them all, the Devil. Now his ultimate desire will soon become reality and his children Alex and Lucy will rule the earth, extinguishing hope, light and love for all eternity. Armageddon is coming and we're powerless to stop it,' sighs Sam in a tired voice that requires all her energy to speak, as the awesome reality of the task that lies before us suddenly becomes apparent.

We all look at each other and for a few moments succumb to our darkest fears whereby evil wins and good loses.

'We must remember why we were charged with this quest and the reasons why Mallon has been given a second chance for redemption. Ma's words are the key, "God always protects the good and fights the evil". We have His protection and He's guided us well so far and will to the end. We must trust in Him and our faith in each other and victory will be ours,' I say, finally understanding why I was given these powerful psychic powers and the gift of 'clear seeing'. It was meant to be. My destiny was written before I was born: to release my father's soul from eternal darkness along with the souls of Shane Colby and the once magnificent Archangel Michael, God's mighty protector. My future was foretold; that the RING and I battle with the darkest demon of all, the Devil, and destroy his children Alex and Lucy, the seeds of pure evil.

'How can we stop the funeral? We don't even know where it's going to be, and what if they bury him back in America?' Robyn asks despondently.

I ponder for a moment and then suddenly it becomes clear. 'We don't have to stop the funeral. We just have to delay it. Remember, the contract is only fulfilled when Mallon's body is claimed by the Enchanter at precisely ten-thirty on the first of June. Therefore even one minute after that time would break the contract, releasing the three souls trapped inside. Also time is running out for them so they'll bury him here in England and that's when we'll strike.'

Immediately Monty and Jack become animated at the thought that maybe there's a glimmer of light at the end of this dark tunnel. 'What exactly do you mean by delaying the funeral, spud? Are you saying that Mallon's body mustn't be buried in the ground at all or that the actual service be delayed until after ten-thirty?' Monty asks excitedly, while Jack quickly chips in. 'What about the Dark Trio, they're not going to let us destroy their plans. Remember we may have the so-called angels of light on our side but they have the Master of Darkness on theirs.'

'Himself will protect us like He's always done,' whispers Aunt Lizzy as she looks behind her shoulders nervously, just in case the spirits of the dark are listening in.

'Well that's OK then. Bring on the beasts, demons, wolf spirits and other creature from Hell, we'll just knock them out one by one,' growls Robyn sarcastically as she desperately tries to hide her inner fears.

'Now, now, everyone, remember we must be together as one, otherwise the Devil and his children will use that weakness within us to break our strength. Besides, we've nothing to lose, for Armageddon is coming and if we don't fight all is lost anyway. We've no choice. Our destiny has already been written,' I say, suddenly feeling incredibly calm and strong as I feel my inner strength returning with a vengeance, igniting my psychic powers to their fullest.

'Sorry, Lizzy, I had a momentary loss of faith but its back now and I'm ready to go into battle,' says Robyn, feeling ashamed and angry with herself for not believing in the RING and our combined psychic powers.

'OK, everyone, listen up, for we need to be prepared,' I announce, feeling an overwhelming sense of freedom, because at last I know who I am. The voices and visions that, as a child I tried to hide because I felt different, I now realise were a divine gift, bestowed upon me so that when Armageddon came I would be ready. 'Firstly, we need to know what's happening with the body and where the funeral is taking place – we already know the date. Robyn, see if your *femme fatale* skills can still work their magic on Sergeant Dredge, as it's a sure bet the police are going to be at the funeral, so they'll know where it's being held.'

'What about Chief Inspector Cranky? Do we tell him what we know?' Robyn asks, now she's back to her old self.

'Don't worry about him. I suspect he'll be nipping at my heels fairly soon to see what I've discovered as they still haven't arrested anybody or even found the murder weapon. While you're busy with Sergeant Dredge, Sam and I will visit the mortuary and chat up Andy, our sniffing psychic friend, as I need to see the body one last time before the Dark Trio take it away for the funeral.'

'Why do you need to see the body again?' asks Sam, rather nervously, as she hadn't anticipated actually seeing the dead body of Mallon, especially after hearing Robyn's gruesome description, and besides, mortuaries aren't exactly on her 'A' list of places to visit.

'It was something Charlotte said when I asked her why she killed her father. She stated that he wasn't dead, but that his body was without blood, lying in a state of catalepsy, waiting for redemption. It's imperative therefore that I put life back into his body again before the Dark Trio bury him.'

'Hang on a minute. Did I just hear you say "put life back into his body"? What do you mean by that exactly and how are you going to do it?' Monty yells, angrily, worried about 'playing God' with life and death.

'Don't worry, honey, I'm not going to create a monster like Frankenstein, I just need to add a tiny pinprick of blood to his cataleptic body. That's all.'

'What do mean, that's all? Whose blood are we talking about here, as if I didn't know and why?' shouts Monty, afraid of what the consequences might be if I mix my blood with that of Mallon.

I slide over and gently put my arms around his strong wide shoulders to comfort and reassure him as I explain. 'In the vision of the healing angels, Archangel Michael was bitten by the Devil disguised as a serpent spreading his poison through his blood to corrupt him. That's why Charlotte drained his body of all its blood. She was trying to purify him of the Devil's poisonous venom. If I can put a drop of my blood into his body then there may be a slim chance that he'll be able to fight against the demons within him when the Devil comes to collect.'

'I'm not sure about this, spud, I don't like the idea of your blood floating around in a demonic corpse.'

'Don't worry, honey, I know what I'm doing, and believe me when I say my pinprick of blood could be the only way that Mallon can achieve redemption, so, my beloved, I need you to be with me on this one,' I beg, using my soft, slightly high-pitched voice, which tends to melt Monty when I want my own way.

'As usual I can't deny you anything, even when I know it's madness,' replies Monty, now melted by my womanly charms.

'Great. Now I need you two handsome hunks to keep a subtle track of the Chief Inspector's moves plus the Dark Trio. Find out what they are up to so we're ready for them this time. Lastly, Lizzy, can you get in contact with Charlotte Mallon and tell her that I now understand the vision of the healing angels, and I'm ready to fulfil my destiny.'

'Why tell his killer what we're doing. Surely you'd be better off telling the police where she is?' says Aunt Lizzy, upset at having to talk to a murderer even if the act was performed out of 'love'.

'Because she's the "Angel of New Beginnings" sent by divine guidance to save not only her father's soul, but the Archangel Michael's and my father's together with all earth's mortal souls from the Devil and his evil offspring, Alex and Lucy. We've the same gifts only hers is that of the angels and more powerful than any mortal's, yet we're bound together through our fathers in the body of Mallon. It's my destiny to join forces with her in the final reckoning to bring about Genesis.'

There follows a seemingly endless silence between us until Robyn chirpily chips in with her usual quirky sense of humour. 'Well I hope there isn't an "Angel of New Beginnings" waiting somewhere out there for me to connect with, unless of course she comes bearing gifts, preferably of the handsome rich male type.'

'To be sure, you've a one track mind, my girl,' Aunt Lizzy giggles as we all chuckle away to ourselves before turning in for an early night to gather our strength, as 1st June draws dangerously close.

'Good morning, you lot, and I hope you've all had a good night's sleep and a hearty breakfast as we've just two days ahead of us before the Devil comes collecting,' I announce as I enter the kitchen and help myself to some scrambled eggs and toast with an extra large mug of strong hot tea, while quietly thinking how lovely it is that Monty's back and Aunt Lizzy foregoes the bedcover stripping routine in the morning. The next 30 minutes evaporate into timelessness as we double check the TIE before setting off on our separate assignments, Robyn to meet Sergeant Dredge, Monty and Jack to track down the Dark Trio and Cranky, Aunt Lizzy to contact Charlotte Mallon, while Sam and I make our way to the mortuary.

'Hello, Miss Holmes, I didn't expect to see you again after your last visit (sniff, sniff). Only one companion this time? (Sniff, sniff.)'

163

'That's right, Andy, meet Sam.'

'Hi, Andy, Charity's told me all about you and how helpful you were to her last time and of your own psychic abilities,' Sam says, appealing to his male ego.

'No trouble at all. Like I said to Miss Holmes, always willing to help a fellow psychic (sniff, sniff),' he replies, hoping that the Dark Trio and Chief Inspector Cranky aren't about to turn up as well.

'We just need to see the body of Mr Mallon once more before the funeral. It won't take but a few minutes,' I say in my ever-so-sweet 'I need your help' voice that men easily succumb to.

'I'm not sure about you viewing the body, Miss Holmes, you know what happened last time when his family arrived (sniff, sniff).'

'Don't worry, Andy, I just need one last look, while you keep a lookout here, and if anybody comes just cough a couple of times and that'll be a signal for Sam and me to hide. Is there another room or store cupboard that we can slip into if the situation necessitates it? You'd be doing a fellow psychic a great favour, which won't be forgotten.'

His eyes dart around the room, fearful that some dark spirit is suddenly about to appear and grab him, while he sniffs continuously, contemplating whether to help us. Eventually his curiosity gets the better of him and he agrees to let us in, pointing to a large walk-in freezer *en route*. 'I can give you five minutes, Miss Holmes (sniff, sniff), and should anyone come in you can hide in the freezer, but you'll only be able to survive for a maximum of ten minutes before your body starts to stiffen (sniff, sniff). After fifteen minutes your organs will begin to fail and within an hour you'll be dead (sniff, sniff),' says Andy as he quickly pulls out Mallon's body, while nervously looking behind him. 'Well, his expression hasn't changed much since the last time you visited (sniff, sniff), and I

164

don't mind admitting that this is one corpse I'll be glad to see the back of, as ever since he's arrived, the place seems to have taken on an eerie feel about it (sniff, sniff).'

As Andy rushes back to the front desk. Sam braces herself and then takes a look at Mallon, shivering and wrapping her arms around her chest, saying, 'Yuck, I see what he means about the expression. He looks terrified and sort of ghoulish at the same time. I wouldn't want to be in his shoes when he meets his maker. I'm not surprised he's asked for your help.'

Then, as Sam loses her fear of dead bodies and starts looking closer into his face, his eyes flicker and his right hand grabs hold of her wrist. She screams, frantically trying to pull away, but his grip is so tight that she's unable to pull free as he draws her down closer to him. 'Oh, my God. Oh, my God, help me, Charity, he's got me. Do something, don't just stand there, ah ... this isn't happening to me,' she cries hysterically.

'Don't panic. Don't panic. Stay very still and very calm. Nothing's going to happen to you. Just listen to the message.'

'What message? I don't want to hear any message. I'm no psychic. Let him give it to you,' screams Sam, who by now is almost hyperventilating as she tries to pull away, only to find his grip getting tighter, while he pulls her so close that their bodies almost touch. I bend over, putting my arms around her, pulling her body into mine until our heads lock together, hovering over Mallon's face, looking deep into his hollow black eyes. I whisper into Sam's ear, 'Don't move. Stay completely still and you'll be fine.' Then, suddenly, Mallon's mouth moves and we hear his pitiful cries. 'Hurry, Charity, time's running out. Save us. Save us.' Then his eyes open wide showing a vision of the Dark Trio walking towards us and instantly I know they're here. He releases his grip on Sam. 'Quick,

165

Sam, into the freezer before they come,' I say as I push Mallon's body back into storage and grab Sam's arm, dragging her across the room and into the freezer just seconds before we hear Andy cough and the Dark Trio arrive.

'I can't believe this, first I'm in mortal danger from a ghoulish corpse, now I'm freezing to death in a mortuary freezer. Forget Armageddon, just get me out of here, Charity,' Sam yells as we try to keep warm by wrapping some blood-stained white sheets thrown in the corner of the freezer around us.

'Hush, Sam, be quiet, they're here and we mustn't give ourselves away,' I whisper as the Dark Trio walk into the room with Andy nervously looking around him, while pulling out Mallon's body.

'Here we are, Mrs Mallon (sniff, sniff). Your husband is still here and I can assure you that no one has attempted to take his body away (sniff, sniff).'

'Are you positive about that, you worm, for I'm certain there's been someone here not long before us?' snarls Alex in that cold voice of his, which sends shudders down your spine and leaves you feeling unclean all over.

'Absolutely, Mr Mallon, only authorised visitors are allowed to view the bodies (sniff, sniff) and as you can see there's no one here (sniff, sniff), and if there were you'd have to pass them in the corridor on their way out (sniff, sniff).' Andy retorts quickly in an unusually brave tone of voice for such a nervous little man, which has raised my opinion of him considerably.

'You can leave us now as we wish a few minutes alone with our father before the funeral,' Lucy says sharply, standing there cold and emotionless, waving her hand at Andy, dismissing him like a worthless nonentity.

'Perhaps it would be better to view your father in a kinder setting such as the funeral parlour (sniff, sniff),

166

where they can make him look more like his old self (sniff, sniff),' suggests Andy nervously, trying not to look over at the slightly opened freezer in the corner where Sam and I are beginning to feel our bodies stiffen from the cold.

'We don't need the opinions of worthless creatures like you on where or when to view our father's body. Now leave us alone,' replies Alex sarcastically, while smirking and staring at Andy in that evil way of his.

Bravely, and to my surprise, Andy retorts, 'Well, that's your decision (sniff, sniff), but I require details of the undertakers and funeral arrangements (sniff, sniff) in order to arrange for collection of his body and finalisation of his papers etc. Oh, and of course, none of this can be done without informing the police (sniff, sniff), being a murder case and all (sniff, sniff). So if you could let me have the information before you leave (sniff, sniff) within the next five minutes, as the mortuary will be closing (sniff, sniff).' With that Andy swiftly returns to his desk without glancing over to the freezer.

'Good old Andy, we may be able to find out where the funeral is. I'm beginning to warm to this little chap. He's quite spunky in a weird sort of way,' I whisper to Sam as the two of us huddle together by the freezer door, listening to the Dark Trio.

'If we don't get out of here soon we'll be joining Mallon in the coffin and I'm not ready for the afterlife yet,' Sam snaps, barely able to open her mouth as she feels her body beginning to stiffen, while I pray that Andy's ploy about closing the mortuary within the next five minutes will save us.

'Father, soon the three souls from this worthless shell will be yours and the power of darkness will descend upon the earth,' says Alex as he raises his arms in the air, while Lucy and Nancy hold hands, looking down at

167

Mallon's body, smiling coldly. Suddenly everything goes black and we hear the voice of pure evil seeping through the walls into the room with that dark, demonic laugh that rips through your soul like a dagger willing you to come to him into the void of eternal damnation.

'My children, the time has come when I, the one true god will invoke the power of darkness upon the earth and you and your children's children will spread my seed amongst these mortals, devouring their souls. Tomorrow at the appointed hour light will be extinguished for all eternity and retribution against He that disowned me into the darkness will be mine. His beloved Archangel Michael's soul will burn in the fires of hell and his power will be mine. Go, my children, and prepare for my coming.'

Then his laugh shrills through my ears until I feel them almost ready to burst as the freezer door suddenly slams shut and we hear him say, 'If only you'd come to me willingly, Charity, your powers would have been infinite. Now your soul, together with your father's, will be mine and I shall welcome you and yours into my kingdom tomorrow... ' As his evil laugh fades into nothingness, Sam and I are trapped in the freezer, so frozen that we're unable to move, awaiting our fate. We hold hands and try to smile at each other, hoping against hope that our God will save us as our eyes slowly begin to close and darkness descends upon us.

'They're still breathing,' are the distant words I hear as I feel my body being lifted into the air and carried effortlessly. I know this voice; it's Chief Inspector Cranky.

'Hurry, we must get them wrapped in foil before it's too late (sniff, sniff),' Andy says, panicking, placing our bodies in the special heat-retaining foil.

As I hear the faint sounds of familiar voices floating

around me I find myself in a dream-like state where Ma and my father (who's so handsome) are smiling down at me, holding hands. Their voices gently whisper in the air, comforting me, 'Don't worry, my precious darling, we're here. Have faith and remember, you've the power of divine guidance, believe in its truth.'

'They're coming round (sniff, sniff). Here we are, Miss Holmes, drink some of this and you'll be fine (sniff, sniff),' are the soft words I hear as I open my eyes to see Andy, Chief Inspector Cranky, Sergeant Dredge, Monty, Jack, Robyn and Aunt Lizzy peering over me as I ask desperately, 'Where's Sam, is she OK?' I am terrified that my dearest friend has been taken by the Devil.

'I'm here, Charity, and I'm fine, but mortuaries are definitely off my list from now on.'

As I feel Monty's strong arms around me and life begins to flow back into my body, I notice that Mallon's corpse is missing. 'Where's Mallon's body and why are you all here?'

They all look at each other in such a way that I sense they're about to tell me they've experienced something phenomenal, as Aunt Lizzy begins...

'I was on the telephone to Charlotte Mallon, giving her your message, when suddenly she interrupts me saying that you and Sam are in trouble and that I must contact the others immediately. Then the line goes dead and before I can dial Monty's number it rings again and he's on the line.'

Monty takes over the story... 'That's right, spud, Jack and I were at Scotland Yard, tracking down the Chief Inspector when suddenly I felt a cold shiver run through me and I had this overwhelming urge to ring you, but every time I rang your mobile the line was dead.'

Then Chief Inspector Cranky interrupts, 'Yeah and while your husband was downstairs trying to contact you

I was in a meeting when I heard this woman's voice from out of nowhere telling me that you were in mortal danger and that your husband was downstairs and I must go to him immediately. I looked around the room to see if anybody else was hearing voices, but they appeared normal. The voice got louder and louder until I jumped off my seat, screaming "shut up" when, at that precise moment, the desk sergeant interrupted the meeting saying that your husband was downstairs and getting into a frantic panic. I rushed down to meet him to find Sergeant Dredge and your secretary arriving at the same time.'

Robyn then takes over. 'Glen and I were having lunch at a nearby restaurant when I heard the same voice. It was a woman's voice, young and very soft, whispering, "Charity and Sam are in danger. You've no time to waste. Collect Monty and the others and get to the mortuary. Hurry, time is running out." I looked at Glen and could see he didn't hear her but I knew who she was – it was Charlotte, so I grabbed his arm and we ran back to the Yard to find Monty and Jack trying to contact you.'

'That's right, spud, I still couldn't get hold of you so rang Aunt Lizzy, who told me what Charlotte had said to her, so we all rushed to the mortuary where we found Andy knocked unconscious at the desk.'

Andy continues. 'When they pulled me round, Miss Holmes (sniff, sniff), I immediately told them about the freezer, which was locked from the outside (sniff, sniff) and to cap it all they'd stolen the body (sniff, sniff).'

I smile at Andy and the others, knowing that my dream as I was being carried out of the freezer, was real. I must trust in my gift and the angels of light who are guiding me towards my destiny.

'What do we do now? They've stolen Mallon's corpse so we've no idea where they're going to bury him and you haven't had the chance to mix your blood with his.

We've only a few hours left before Armageddon. That's it, it's all over, we're doomed,' cries Sam as we all stand motionless in the middle of the mortuary surrounded by dead bodies, contemplating our next move.

'Let us all lock hands in a circle, forming a ring of power to enable Robyn and me to channel our powers to their fullest and seek out the Dark Trio,' I say gently, gathering everyone together, and as we form our RING I recite Psalm 23 from the Book of David knowing that our Lord will send us a sign.

'1. The Lord is my shepherd; I shall not want.
2. He maketh me to lie down in green pastures:
   He leadeth me beside the still waters.
3. He restoreth my soul:
   He guideth me in the paths of righteousness for his name's sake.
4. Yea, though I walk through the valley of the shadow of death,
   I will fear no evil; for thou art with me.
   Thy rod and thy staff, they comfort me.
5. Thou preparest a table before me in the presence of mine enemies:
   Thou hast anointed my head with oil: my cup runneth over.
6. Surely goodness and mercy shall follow me all the days of my life:
   And I will dwell in the house of the Lord for ever.'

As I pray, a golden light descends into the centre of the RING, forming a beam of pure energy that opens up into the sky and beyond until we're floating in a sea of pure love. We feel its warmth penetrating our bodies, engulfing us in its purity, while we float higher and higher

171

until our bodies feel weightless and the most wonderful feeling of complete love overwhelms us. Then we see him descend into the beam of light: God's mighty Archangel Focus, who has the power of infallible thought. As he descends, we see the splendour of his magnificent golden brown wings stretched high above him, which fold around us, forming a shield. His body is completely covered in golden brown feathers that shimmer in the light, almost blinding us with their purity. He raises his left hand high above his head, while he lowers his sword of justice in his right hand until it is on my forehead. His voice echoes all around, cocooning us in its power.

'I am the gatekeeper of infallible thought, which I bring to you, Charity. Feel its power and know the infallible mind of God, as it enters your thoughts through the sword of justice and opens the doorway that leads you to your destiny.'

I feel his sword burning through my thoughts, reaching into the depths of my mind until the doorway to the 'third eye' is opened. I see a dark Gothic church standing high on a hill, hidden behind huge black gates with a tall pointed steeple reaching up into the sky. There are grey buildings beneath the hill. Flying dragon skeletals (evil grey transparent skeletal dragon spirits that were once mythical fire-breathing monsters, until the Devil captured their souls and became their Master) swoop up and around the steeple. They come only when death is your fate, sent by the Lord of Darkness to breathe the fires of Hell upon you. Never look into the eyes of these flying skeletal monsters for you'll see your soul burning in Hell. A mighty wind howls and the sky opens up into black, acid rain, which if it touches your skin penetrates deep into your mind, feeding you the dark thoughts of the Devil, until you go mad. I look closer and see a name carved in red upon the gates: 'NODDEGAMRA'. The

172

church bells ring one by one until they reach ten, when the earth beneath crumbles inwards, forming an endless dark cavity that leads to the 'dark life', whose ruler is the Lord of Darkness, the Devil.

Suddenly the doorway to the 'third eye' is closed and I see no more, as I return to the RING and the golden light of Focus. I look across the circle and see Robyn's eyes and know that she feels my terror as I saw the beginning of the rebirth of the Devil. I feel the mighty sword of justice lift from my forehead as Focus slowly rises up, spreading his wings so high and wide that they eclipse the sky, while the RING descends to the ground.

As we look up into the golden beam of light and see the magnificent Archangel floating above, looking down upon us, we feel the power of his voice charge through our bodies like an electric shock.

'Use the power of infallible thought to focus your mind, Charity, and you'll see where your destiny lies.'

Suddenly the beam of pure light begins to fade as he disappears into the heavens, leaving us once more back in the coldness of the mortuary with the RING still unbroken. As I follow the faces around the circle I smile at what I see: the oh-so-stiff Chief Inspector Cranky speechless and white with shock, with his sidekick Sergeant Dredge mummified and twitchless; Andy sniffless for once, while the rest of the RING slowly feel their bodies returning to them.

'Well, I suppose that's what you'd call experiencing something phenomenal, Miss Holmes, only this time I can't explain it away,' says a dazed and humbled Chief Inspector.

Andy, too, finds his voice. 'Wait until I tell them about this at the Inner Light Psychic Group's monthly meeting – they'll never top this (sniff, sniff).'

'Inner Light Psychic Group, now I've heard it all,' laughs the Chief Inspector as he suddenly finds he has a sense

173

of humour. We all make our way back to Andy's office and help ourselves to whatever drinks we can find.

'What did you see when Focus placed his sword on your forehead? I felt your terror but my powers aren't strong enough to open the doorway into the "third eye",' Robyn asks, quickly downing a glass of beer that she has found in Andy's personal fridge.

'I saw the place where they've taken Mallon's body and I now know its secret. It's a dark Gothic church with a tall pointed steeple that almost touches the sky. It stands high on a hill, hidden behind huge black gates with the name of the church carved in red on them. Its name is "NODDEGAMRA",' I reply, feeling a cold shiver run through me as I say it out loud.

'That's a really strange name for a church, spud? Yet it sounds familiar, somehow,' Monty replies suddenly feeling rather cold.

I draw my breath for a few seconds before enlightening him. 'That's because its Armageddon spelt backwards.' There's an eerie silence as everyone begins to realise that their lives have been touched by divine decree, with their fates already predetermined. The silence is broken when Jack asks the question that everyone is thinking, 'Did you see where this church is and can we get there in time?' As everyone's eyes are upon me I feel like the Grim Reaper sending them to their fates, yet I have no choice but to tell them.

'It's in a place called KRADLIVED, somewhere deep in the moorlands of Dartmoor, which used to be a village hundreds of years ago until it was destroyed by fire. Legend has it that the people who lived there were evil heathens who worshipped the Lord of Darkness. It's said that they performed pagan ceremonies in a church they built on a hill near the town, the church Focus showed me through the doorway of the third eye, NODDEGAMRA.

174

'During their pagan ceremonies, history tells of them sacrificing children, whose souls had to be pure and devoid of all evil. As time went on it became harder for them to find pure children amongst their own so they began to search wider, stealing children from other villages and towns, yet nothing could be proven against them. Then one day they stole and sacrificed the child of a prominent clergyman called Nollam – Mallon backwards – who lived in a town called Nevaeh – Heaven, backwards – one hundred and fifty miles away. He was bereft at the loss of his son, so with an army of men rode through the night until they arrived in the morning at the village of Kradlived – Dark Devil backwards – where they burnt it to the ground along with all its men, women and children until all that was left was black ash. They tried to burn down the church, but it's said that the skies opened up, bringing forth black acid rain, which sent them into madness and eventually a slow and agonising death.

'The date and time of this terrible dark deed was the first of June at ten-thirty in the morning. I now see that Mallon's death was predestined. He was meant to die in England so that the Dark Trio could use his shell of a body to perform a sacrificial ceremony in the pagan church of NODDEGAMRA. From that first meeting at my seminar in South Carolina when our eyes met and the connection was made, to his death and subsequent materialisation in spirit, all of our fates have been predestined to lead us to the final reckoning at Kradlived.'

I stop for a few minutes to take a drink, for my mouth is dry and my heart heavy with sadness as I look around and see the horror on each of their faces, as they realise what pure evil has predetermined their fates.

'The Lord of Darkness will be reborn in his village, Kradlived, where his disciples were destroyed by those

175

who lived in the town of Nevaeh by sacrificing the three souls he stole. The first belonged to an innocent boy, Shane Colby, who was pure and devoid of all evil, as were the children sacrificed in the church of NODDEGAMRA. The second soul was that of Archangel Michael, God's mighty protector from Heaven. The third was the soul of my father, which possessed the powerful gifts I was destined by divine guidance to inherit – the power to intercept between the living here on earth and those in spirit, combined with the gift of "clear seeing", that has shown me my destiny, which is to prevent his coming. He must destroy me before I get to Mallon's body and can destroy him, but my father's gift still remains with him even in spirit and he, along with the angels, has guided and protected me so that I can fulfil my destiny.'

The silence between us is almost deafening with its screams of despair and fear as everyone contemplates the epic battle that lies ahead and the terrible consequences should we fail. Eventually it's Sergeant Dredge who breaks the silence by asking, without even one twitch, 'Well, I hate to point out the obvious, but how are we going to get to Kradlived in time to destroy this demon?' To which Chief Inspector Cranky surprisingly suggests, 'By helicopter of course, but where the hell are going to find one at this time of night?' Then all eyes turn to Jack as we suddenly realise he's the man with the military connections.

'OK. OK, I guess this could be classed a state emergency, but somehow explaining to my army buddies that the world's going to be destroyed by a demon in a few hours isn't going to do it,' replies Jack, frantically trying to think of a way around it when Monty has a brainwave.

'We can do it. Sam, ring your husband – he's a High Court Judge – and get him to fax a signed authorisation requesting two helicopters to my boss John Henderson, head of Special Operations at the Secret Service. While you are doing that I'll contact him direct so he can be ready to fax it along with his added authorisation for additional men and weaponry to Jack's contacts in the Army Special Forces, requesting them to collect us from here *en route* to Kradlived.' Jack quickly gets on his mobile informing his old SAS buddies at Army Special Forces to be ready.

Suddenly I remember the black rain. 'Don't forget the black rain,' I shout. 'We need special protective clothing otherwise we'll all be destroyed.'

'Add special protective clothing against acid to that list, John,' Monty says quickly as he finishes talking to his boss at Special Operations.

I look at Cranky, Dredge and Andy and ask myself, 'Do I have the right to send them into battle?' But then it's their fight as much as mine so I offer them the choice to decide their own destiny. 'You don't have to come, you know. You've done enough already, my friends.'

All three look at each other and smile as Andy replies, 'We're sticking with you, Miss Holmes (sniff, sniff). After all, you're the one with the gift and the protection of the angels (sniff, sniff).'

Then Aunt Lizzy says proudly, 'Don't yah be forgetting "Himself" as well, for he's all powerful and has been watching over my Charity since the day she was born. He'll not let any harm come to her or her family.'

We all separate to different parts of the mortuary to reflect, say some private prayers and speak to our loved ones for maybe the last time. Cranky telephones his wife, Dredge his mother and brother, Andy his friend and companion, Jack, well he continues to play it cool as Sam telephones Leo again, while Robyn and Aunt Lizzy reminisce together. Monty and I sneak off to a dark corner and, well, enough said there.

Then we hear the sound of helicopters!

177

* * *

As we fly over the mystical moorlands with their dark, shadowy hills, whispering winds and hidden secrets, searching for the pagan church NODDEGAMRA and the lost village Kradlived, I look around at my friends and loved ones all dressed in their protective clothing, army helmets and weapons (which will be powerless against the evil that we're about to face) and I quietly pray to my God and protector to see us safely through this battle. Then, as the skies become lighter, we begin to descend lower upon the moors, while the pilot desperately searches for the hill where Armageddon is calling. 'Come in Red Dog eleven; Red Dog one calling, what's your position and anything to report?' The radio crackles and hisses as we hear the faint voice of the pilot in the other helicopter reporting.

'Red Dog eleven reporting. We're over a place called Draklevid Gorge, but no sighting of a church yet, Red Dog one. Will keep you posted, over.'

Everyone checks their watches; its 9.45 a.m. and a cold chill runs through our bodies, knowing that time is rapidly running out.

'I'm not sure what we're supposed to be looking for here, Jack, let's just hope it's not a wild goose chase for I'd hate to have to explain all this manpower and machinery away to the "big nobs" above should nothing come of it,' shouts the SAS commander over the noise of the helicopter rotor blades to Jack, seated at the other end surrounded by more SAS Special Troops, all kitted out for war.

'Don't worry, Mac, if we don't find it before ten-thirty it isn't going to matter,' replies Jack, looking anxiously over at the rest of us.

As we continue to fly over the moors a deadly silence descends upon us as we all try not to look at each other,

178

each quietly feeling our stomachs churning and our throats dry with a combination of fear and panic; fear if we should find NODDEGAMRA and panic if we don't. Either way, the waiting is unbearable. I check my watch; it's now 9.58. Then it happens...

'Come in, Red Dog one; Red Dog eleven calling; code red, code red. Oh my God. Oh my God. I don't believe what I'm seeing; this isn't real. We're under attack, repeat we're under attack. Need assistance, code red, repeat code red.'

Our pilot responds as the commander stands by. 'Red Dog one calling, over. Where's your position, Red Dog eleven? Repeat, give us your position, Red Dog eleven, over.' Then the commander grabs the pilot's radio.

'Red Dog one, Commander Machinney here, who's attacking you? Give details, over. Repeat, who's attacking you, over?' Our pilot leaves the radio channel open for a response, but what we hear are the cries of men entering the eternal abyss of darkness.

'Come in, Red Dog one, can you hear us? We're under attack, repeat, we're under attack, code red, repeat, code red. Oh my God, they're everywhere, hundreds of them. They look like flying skeletons with wings breathing black flames. They're on the helicopter; Jesus, they're huge dragons with no flesh; they've got the rotor blades. We're going down, I repeat, we're going down. God help us – they're coming in, they're coming in. Their eyes. Oh my God, their eyes. Help us; help me; I see me; I see me. Oh, the despair, the darkness, the pain. God help me; please help me; no, don't take me, please don't...'

As we hear their last cries of despair the silence amongst us screams our feelings of impotence and powerlessness. Then as we pull ourselves together the commander asks the pilot to check on the map for the location of Draklevid Gorge (Red Dog 11's last sighting before they went down), while I look at Monty and the others. 'What is it, spud? I recognise that look; you know something,' Monty says, almost afraid to hear the answer.

'The name Draklevid Gorge – its KRADLIVED.'

Everyone sits frozen for a few moments as we all realise that we've reached our destiny. I check my watch; it's 10.08. 'We mustn't fly over the gorge, Commander, or our fate will be that of Red Dog eleven. We need to land a safe distance from it and make our way on foot, camouflaged within the moors, praying that the dragon skeletals don't spot us.'

We make our way through the grass, heather and moss of the moors on foot, and as we draw closer we crawl on our stomachs until we reach the edge of the gorge. The commander signals his men to spread out, while Monty and I, together with Jack, Robyn, Aunt Lizzy, Sam, Cranky, Dredge and Andy look on. What we see is the reality of my vision, shown to me by Focus through the power of infallible thought and the doorway to the 'third eye'. It's not a valley, but the resurrection of the village of Kradlived looked over and dominated by its pagan church with its huge black gates, upon which its name is written in blood – NODDEGAMRA. The earth beneath is black like soot (the ashes of the hundreds of dead souls waiting to be resurrected), upon which are the charcoal remains of their village. The church is dark and Gothic, with its walls crumbled so we can see into its soul, while its steeple is surrounded by flying dragon skeletals, swooping in and out, breathing their black flames of death.

Then in its soul we see the Dark Trio conducting their

180

ritual as they stand in a circle around a sacrificial alter upon which lays the body of Mallon. Alex wears ram horns (symbol of Satan) upon his head, with his arms raised high in the air holding the red and black staff of Lucifer (to open the doorway into the 'dark life') in his left hand, as Lucy and Nancy complete the circle, dressed in black hooded robes. We can hear Alex calling to his father as Lucy and Nancy recite their demonic prayers to complete the circle of death and await the coming of their father the Lord of Darkness.

The bells begin to ring as the skies turn black, bringing forth the black acid rain as the earth beneath crumbles inwards into the endless black cavity I saw in my vision. From within this black hole they come forth to protect their Master and await his coming. There are hundreds of them. They rise up and fly into the black skies and rain, joining forces with the dragon skeletals as they swoop in and out and around NODDEGAMRA and the dead village of Kradlived. I turn and look at Monty (while gripping his hand tightly) and the others to see their tortured expressions of horror and fear at what they see, some with their mouths open in disbelief, but all silent and still with the pale complexion of terror. Even I, Charity Holmes, the Inceptor can hardly believe the evil that's before me. Evil spirits, demons, fallen angels and monsters come forth from Hell in their multitudes. Some we've already fought in our quest to get here and others I've never seen: **Evil wolf spirits** (who eat ravenously on your body); the **beast** (scaly red horned reptile breathing the fires of Hell); **two-headed serpents** (one bite corrupts your soul); **winged wraiths** (fallen angels wielding their swords of death – one strike through your heart seals your fate); **lost souls** (those taken without warning including the men on Red Dog 11); **evil spirits** (the damned souls of the village of Kradlived destroyed by fire and the town of Nevaeh, whose transparent bodies show the ravages of acid rain); and finally, the **Knight of Death** (a black armoured knight – a skeleton – who rides upon his white skeletal horse carrying the black flag of death. Should he ride towards you and touch your head with his flag then death is your prize.)

Then the final bell rings (the tenth) and he rises from beneath his kingdom: the Lord of Darkness in his true form, the **Horned Goat of Mendes** – half man, half beast, horned and tailed with the dark Satanic eyes of the Devil, his great black bat wings flapping backwards and forwards, lifting him upwards until he emerges from the 'dark life', hovering over his children and servants, eclipsing all light. As he looks down upon the Dark Trio and Mallon's body we hear that black demonic voice, which echoes throughout the moors until it pierces our ears with its evil words.

'I, the ONE TRUE GOD, now invoke the POWER OF DARKNESS upon the earth and claim what is MINE.'

Then he reaches down and touches Alex's staff with his hand, igniting its power as it metamorphoses into a huge black serpent with a long red forked tongue and sharp, pointed yellow teeth. All his servants swoop down and around Mallon's body, screaming their cries of death, while the black rain pours and skies thunder, as Lucy and Nancy bend down and pray to their Lord. Then we hear Mallon's cry of death as his eyes open to see Alex lowering his left hand, bringing the black serpent of death closer to his body. I feel my soul crumble with despair as I look at my watch; it's 10.16, and then glance at the others to see their anguish as we watch hopelessly, unable to stop the inevitable. I can bear it no longer and cry out, 'Lord, why have you forsaken us?' Then I hear her soft golden voice.

'I'm with you, Charity. Come face your destiny.' I feel her hand upon me; **Charlotte Mallon in angel form**. Her magnificent golden wings lift me into the skies as we fly like birds in the wind, while she whispers in my ear, 'Look behind you, Charity, and see the power of God.' As we fly towards Armageddon through the black rain, protected by our special clothing, I look back to see a **golden army of angels** flying behind us, carrying my loved ones, friends and soldiers beneath them. It is an army of: **archangels** (Sovereign, Focus, Freedom, Friendship, Power and Strength wielding their swords of justice in their right hands, as they carry Monty and my loved ones in their left); **guardian angels** (Retreat, Support, Surrender, Trust and Truth with their magnificent green and grey wings and their ability to breathe the white flames of protection); and **healing angels** (Harmony, Inspiration, Listening, Miracles and Serenity, who can heal with one touch of their right hand). Finally I see the **angels of divine guidance** (an army of them with their bows and arrows, which can destroy any enemy with one deadly shot).

Then, as I turn round, I see Armageddon flying towards us as the Lord of Darkness sends his army of servants to protect him and his children as the **battle begins**.

They come at us from all directions, as our army of angels go into battle, destroying them one by one. Wolf spirits fly towards the commander and his soldiers to tear at their flesh, but they're destroyed by the flying arrows of the angels of divine guidance (who are carrying them under their wings), while I see the beast trying to breathe the fires of Hell upon Monty, who's quickly defended by the guardian angel Truth as he breathes the white flames of protection upon the beast and he disintegrates into the black rain. The two-headed serpent slithers towards Sam as it lashes out its long black forked tongue to strike her down and take her soul, but just as it's upon her the archangel Strength (who's carrying her under his wings) wields his mighty sword of justice, cutting through its head so it tumbles back into the pit of darkness from whence it came.

I see the army of lost souls (transparent white figures of their mortal bodies) surrounding Jack, Robyn and Aunt Lizzy (who are being carried by archangels Freedom, Power and Sovereign), as they weave amongst them trying to corrupt their thoughts with their evil cries and taunts, but the guardian angels Retreat, Support and Surrender fly to their defence, breathing their white flames of protection upon Jack, Robyn and Aunt Lizzy so that nothing can enter their bodies or minds to corrupt them.

As we draw closer to our destiny, winged wraiths fly towards Cranky and Dredge (who are being carried by archangels Focus and Friendship), wielding their swords of death as they attempt to strike them through the heart. But the angels battle it out with their swords until Focus and Friendship each wield one fatal strike from their mighty swords of justice through the hearts of the wraiths, destroying them as they crumble into dust. The evil spirits of the damned try to grab Andy (who's being carried by the Angel of Divine Guidance) and pull him down into their world, but the healing angels, Harmony, Inspiration, Listening and Serenity fly towards him, forming a 'ring of defence' so no harm can come to him. Then, just as I'm about to come face to face with the Lord of Darkness, the Knight of Death rides towards me, stretching out his black flag of death (while Alex rises up and pulls Charlotte to the ground), touching my forehead as I tumble down onto the body of Mallon, who lies frozen with his eyes wide open awaiting the deadly bite of the black serpent of death, which is almost upon him as 10.30 a.m. is but a few seconds away.

* * *

As I lay upon Mallon's body, slowly drifting into the sleep
of eternal darkness, I see the black serpent of death
coming down upon us and the evil faces of Alex, Lucy
and Nancy smiling with their Master and father, the Devil,
who's laughing his demonic cries of victory as the bells
ring out for one last time and 10.30 a.m. has come.
Then, just as I feel my eyes close, I look around to see
the pain and anguish on my beloved Monty's face as he
and the others stand with their angels over them looking
down on me as the black serpent of death sinks his teeth
into Mallon and then me and I feel all my strength and
light leaving my body as evil wins and good loses.

Just as I feel the last breath of life leaving me there's
a hand upon my forehead, which burns through my mind,
body and soul until I feel life growing within me. I begin
to breathe again and can hear the soft voice of angels
whispering in my ears as I slowly open my eyes to look
upon the most magnetic of visions: an angel – a beautiful
blue healing angel with long flowing jet-black hair,
magnificent emerald-green wings that curve around her
body, enveloping me in them, and dressed in midnight-
blue robes with a golden flame burning from her fingers.
She whispers, 'Rise up, Charity, as I, God's most powerful
healing angel, Miracle, return the "flame of life" back
into your soul, giving you the "powerful light of the
angels".'

As I awake from the 'sleep of death' I feel myself
floating in the air, while above, Miracle protects me from
the Dark Trio and their Master by enveloping me completely
in her soft emerald-green wings as she continues to
whisper, 'Take your blood and give it to the three souls,
releasing them from darkness.'

I feel the warm blood trickling down my neck where

the black serpent of feath has sunk his teeth into me. I look down upon Mallon's body, as I float above him with Miracle, who protects us both from the evil above. Instinctively, I lower my head until it's face to face with Mallon's as I let my blood trickle into the bite on his neck, mixing the two bloods together so that powerful light of the angels now flows through his body.

Within moments his body metamorphoses one by one into: Shane Colby, Archangel Michael and finally my father, as it glows with the brightest of lights, and I look upon the most handsome of men aged about thirty with bright-blue sparking eyes, blond hair and the most magnetic of smiles. As we look into each other's eyes, I see me. I see who I am. I see my destiny and I feel complete. Then I feel my body, together with my father's, rising higher and higher as Miracle carries both of us (cradled under her wings) up into the heavens until we're looking down upon NODDEGAMRA and Kradlived. The black rain ceases, revealing a magnificent rainbow whose colours beam down on the entire village and everyone in it. Then we hear the voice of the most powerful angel of all, the One True Being, God, an indescribable voice emitting immeasurable power and unbounded love, which completely fulfils you until your whole body feels weightless in its purity.

'There is only ONE. I am HE. Know who I am and you shall know PEACE. Follow the LIGHT and no harm shall beset thee for I am HE, the giver of life.'

As He speaks, the skies open up, bringing forth hundreds of beams of light through the rainbow, down upon all the evil spirits, demons and beasts, destroying them one by one as they desperately try to escape their fate, while screaming to their Master to protect them. Their master flies up into the heavens spreading his huge bat wings high above him as he tries to destroy my father and me.

186

But before he can reach us Archangel Michael metamorphoses from within my father's body, wielding his mighty sword as he flies towards the Devil with his magnificent wings spreading out high and wide above him, flapping back and forth in the heavens as the two battle fearlessly, Michael with his sword and the golden light of God protecting him; the Devil with his horns, tail and claw feet encompassed in the black flames of Hell. His children and Nancy look up in hatred and fear as the battle with the angels of light, the RING, my friends and soldiers continues to rage around them with the beams of light destroying any evil it touches.

Slowly good wins as the angels, Monty, my loved ones, friends and soldiers (with the help of God's beaming light) destroy all the Devil's servants until there's only Alex, Lucy and Nancy left, as their Master continues to battle with the mighty Archangel Michael. The Devil lashes out with his horns and claw feet as his great black bat wings clash with Michael's in the heavens, but nothing can penetrate God's golden light, even when the Devil tries to breathe the flames of Hell upon it. Below, Alex can see that his father is losing, so raises his hands in the air and speaks the tongues of Beelzebub to bring forth the flying flames of death (arrow-shaped flames of fire that speed through the air, seeking out their victims like missiles) from the 'dark life' to seek out Michael and destroy him.

But as the flaming missiles shoot up from beneath the earth and fly towards Michael, Charlotte (who's lying on the ground, hurt) rises up, flying towards him with the 'dagger of requital', which she used to 'kill' her father, in her right hand. One strike from an angel, wielding God's golden dagger, with the sign of the cross carved into its ivory handle, emblazoned with precious jewels, brings final retribution upon his enemies. Charlotte raises the dagger and stabs him through the heart.

Instantly the missiles disintegrate, just before they reach their target, as Alex is collected by the dark spirits of death (evil black spirits that crawl up from the 'dark life'), who take him back down with them to the darkness and an eternity of torment as he cries out in despair. Lucifer turns and looks down to see his 'son' destroyed as Michael wields his sword of justice down upon his head, striking through his horns and body until he splits into two, falling back down into the pit of darkness from whence he came.

As the Lord of Darkness returns to his kingdom, the ground closes up, taking all his remaining evil servants with him, finally culminating with Lucy and Nancy, who desperately try to avoid their fate by clinging to the pillars of the church. They cry their screams of terror before finally succumbing to their fate and are carried away by the dark spirits of death down into the 'dark life' for all eternity.

Archangel Michael spreads his wings high into the heavens, while encircling us in his protective light, as he gently lowers my father and me back down to Draklevid Gorge until we're standing by Monty as the earth closes beneath us, returning the ground once more to the peaceful green lands of the moors.

13

Genesis

As I stand with Monty, surrounded by Robyn, Sam, Aunt Lizzy, Jack, Cranky, Dredge, Andy, Commander Machinney, his soldiers and our army of golden angels, we see the heavens open up, bringing forth an illumination of golden blue and white flames that radiate the powerful light of God throughout the skies. We watch in wonder as our Lord, the giver of life and His children descend, while Charlotte and Archangel Michael spread their magnificent wings and fly up into the circle of golden flames to take their place by His side.

I look up at the most glorious of sights. I behold our Lord, the most powerful angel of all in the middle, high above His children, with His magnificent wings of brilliant white in the centre fusing into blues and greens and culminating in one golden light, spread upwards and rising high behind Him, glowing with the flames of life, just as I remember in the vision shown to me by Charlotte. As He descends, Archangel Michael returns to His right side with Focus on His left, both wielding their swords of justice in their right hands. Beside Focus there are three angels, the **Angel of Answered Prayers** (all dressed in white with beautiful white-feathered wings – Mallon's prayers for redemption have been answered); the **Angel of Celebration** (her wings and robes are a fusion of pink

189

and cream to celebrate our victory); and the **Angel of Signs** (a blue vision, which showed us the way to our destiny). Beside Michael I see Charlotte, the **Angel of New Beginnings**, with her father Mallon at her side, now free of the coat of the 'dark life', and replaced by resplendent burgundy wings, holding her hand and smiling, a dark-haired man, whose hollow black eyes and ghoulish face have been replaced by sparkling jet-black eyes and the most handsome of faces, glowing in the light of God. Next to them there's Shane Colby, a handsome boy happily laughing with his parents. Beside them is the **Angel of Freedom**, splendid in his nudity (free from any suppression) and flesh-coloured wings, who has freed his soul from the darkness.

Underneath our Lord I see Ma who has joined my father (now complete with pale blue wings). Both hold hands and smile down upon me as I feel my throat choke, my eyes trickle with the tears of joy, and my heart and soul lifted into brightness, knowing that they're now complete, together at last in the afterlife. Finally, underneath them in the centre, is the **Angel of Forgiveness** (Charlotte's mother) with the 'golden ring of absolution' around her head, majestic as she floats above us with her gold and cream wings spread wide and dressed in golden robes of pure silk, bringing forgiveness and the power of inauguration.

A benevolent silence descends upon the moors as our army of golden angels leave us to join their father in the heavens. They float around the vision of pure love we see before us and then we hear his golden voice...

'Charity, your quest for truth and redemption has been answered. I free you of your charge and give you and your loved ones peace. Your destiny has been fulfilled. I give you the power of the angels, who'll guide you on your life's journey as an inceptor.'

190

Slowly the vision before us disappears into the heavens as Mallon, Charlotte, Shane, Archangel Michael, Ma and my father (whose name I've yet to know) smile and wave to me, while I'm left standing in the pagan church of NODDEGAMRA holding Monty tightly. The RING can breathe again knowing that, this time, the battle between good and evil has been won.

But the war continues...